THE INVENTORY
GRAVITY

Also by Andy Briggs:

The Inventory: Iron Fist

THE INVENTORY
GRAVITY

ANDY BRIGGS

MSCHOLASTIC

Scholastic Children's Books
An imprint of Scholastic Ltd
Euston House, 24 Eversholt Street, London, NW1 1DB, UK
Registered office: Westfield Road, Southam, Warwickshire, CV47 0RA
SCHOLASTIC and associated logos are trademarks and/or
registered trademarks of Scholastic Inc.

First published in the UK by Scholastic Ltd, 2016

Copyright © Andy Briggs, 2016

The right of Andy Briggs to be identified as the author
of this work has been asserted by him.

ISBN 978 1407 16180 8

A CIP catalogue record for this book
is available from the British Library.

Printed by CPI Group (UK) Ltd, Croydon, CR0 4YY

Papers used by Scholastic Children's Books are made
from wood grown in sustainable forests.

1 3 5 7 9 10 8 6 4 2

www.scholastic.co.uk

SAB – A TRUE WONDER OF THE WORLD

AND TO CRUMBS... AN EMPTIER
PLACE WITHOUT YOU...

THE BIG CRUSH

Kardach tickled the Ducati motorbike's throttle, the powerful engine wanting to go faster, but the rider had no desire to be pulled over by the cops.

Kardach glanced at the clock projected on his helmet's visor. He was running late; no surprise there. He eased off the interstate and turned on to a wide boulevard. He was wrapped in thick biker leathers, and a bead of sweat trickled down his forehead. He couldn't wait to take the claustrophobic helmet off.

Not much further. Ahead lay the aging multistorey car park where he was meeting his contact. Kardach indicated his turn, then carefully pulled off the boulevard. He took a ticket from the gate and patiently waited for the barrier to rise. Then he calmly accelerated up the ramp, heading for the fifth floor. No point in drawing attention, he reminded himself.

His contact, a muscular South African man named Christen Sandberg, was impatiently pacing around his huge Cadillac Escalade, and he made a show of looking at his watch when Kardach appeared at the top of the ramp. Christen – more commonly known by a string of murderous nicknames – had been told to come alone. So naturally he came with three shades-wearing bodyguards.

Kardach revved the engine as he pulled up in front of them, the bike's roar echoing around the otherwise empty car park. Kardach cut the engine, climbed off and kicked out the bike's support stand.

"You better have a very good reason for keeping me waiting," snarled Christen in his thick Afrikaans accent.

Kardach pulled off his helmet and sucked in a deep breath to cool himself. He ignored Christen's expectant look. He pulled the case off his bike and lowered it to the floor, the weight almost pulling his arms from their sockets. The metal made a loud thud.

Christen exchanged a puzzled look with his men. "I don't think he can hear me. Are you deaf, man?"

Kardach opened the case and revealed several olive-green plastic parts nestled in foam trays. With practised speed he assembled the components, each sliding into the other with a delicate click. Within seconds he had assembled something that looked like a rifle. He took great care to lock the final component in place: an orb that hung under the barrel.

Christen broke into peals of laughter. "That's it? That's what all the secrecy was about? It looks like a kiddie's water pistol!"

His henchmen joined in his laughter. Kardach grinned and hoisted the plastic rifle with both hands. He pushed the stock against his shoulder, and it took all his strength just to hold the weapon level. Then he playfully aimed it at the laughing thugs.

"I think you have been wasting my time," Kardach said. "I was told your organization was a serious one. Into serious business."

Kardach flipped a switch on the weapon, and it hummed to life. He winked at the South African. Then he pulled the trigger.

He felt the bass wave vibrate his hand, then his shoulder, passing through to his feet before the concrete floor around them shuddered so fiercely that fine cracks snaked out from under him. Still, Kardach stood firm. He knew what to expect.

With a sonorous boom, a wave of blue lights cycled through the plastic barrel. The air shimmered like a heat haze as a stream of clear energy encompassed the car and three thugs. A high-pitched sound could barely be heard as the car began to twist, as if melting. But it wasn't melting; it was constricting in on itself as the atoms forming the car pulled together with unstoppable force.

Within seconds the car crushed itself into a bit of heavy metal the size of a marble. It dropped to the floor with a thud, forming a crater in the concrete.

Kardach deactivated the gun and laid it on the floor to ease his aching arms. Christen stared at what remained of his car in disbelief. It took a few more moments for him to realize that his three bodyguards had vanished.

"Where are my men?"

"They didn't feel a thing. The gravity wave crushed them almost instantly. Your car put up a bit more of a struggle."

Christen tried to pick up his crushed car. It refused to move.

Kardach smirked. "That marble still weighs the same as your car did. It's just super-dense."

Christen regarded Kardach for a moment. Well-built with dark shoulder-length hair framing a lean face, he didn't look overly unusual. However, there was an emptiness in his eyes, and Christen couldn't maintain eye contact for long. He moved his greedy gaze to the weapon on the floor.

"Where did that come from?"

"That doesn't matter. My employer just told me to pass it on to you." Kardach watched Christen walk over and hesitate before crouching to run his hand across the rifle's plastic casing. "And to ensure you follow instructions."

Christen's head snapped up. "What instructions?"

Kardach tossed him a small earpiece. Christen caught it on reflex.

"You'll get them in due time. In the meantime, I'll show you how to use that." He nodded towards the weapon. "They call it Newton's Arrow. The casing is a gravity-resistant polychro-compound. Whatever that means. I just know it's tough stuff. The selector at the side allows you to set the strength of graviton flow—"

"What instructions?" Christen was now standing

and looking at Kardach with suspicion. "I thought this was a gift."

Kardach smiled. "Think of it as a trade. You get a shiny new toy and all you have to do is a few favours."

Christen looked at the crushed car thoughtfully before he spoke again. "This boss of yours, Double Helix. What's he like?"

"Not the kind of person you should mess with. And not a name you should mention. Stick to 'Shadow Helix'; that's the name of the organization. The only name you need to know."

Christen nodded. He struggled to pick up the heavy rifle – Newton's Arrow – huffing with the effort. He weighed it in his hands.

"You better show me how to use it, then," he grinned.

MAN OF ACTION

"Ready?" asked Lot, unable to keep the excitement from her voice.

Dev smiled and grunted in response. The smile was fake, and he hoped Lot couldn't see his nervousness beneath. As the entire aircraft cabin shook around them, his smile dropped, but Lot's just broadened.

"Ten seconds!" yelled Sergeant Wade from the cockpit.

The turbulence was turning Mason's stomach, and he hardly had the strength to hold out the Iron Fist gauntlet, waiting for Dev to slip his hand in.

What a nightmare their first mission was turning

out to be. Mason had spent most of the flight hunched over the cramped toilet being violently ill. Dev had been anxious as he replayed Eema's simulations over and over in his head. And Lot, well, as the daughter of an air force test pilot, she had been bouncing with excitement since they'd first set foot aboard the Eiodolon Drop Fighter.

A warning bell squawked through the aircraft, and seconds later hydraulic pistons lowered the tail ramp. They all jolted from the sudden rush of air. The Eiodolon was slowing down, but it was still flying faster than the speed of sound. Lot and Mason were connected to the ceiling with safety cords, but Dev wasn't, and could feel himself being pulled towards the ramp.

He quickly slid his hand into the Iron Fist gauntlet. He sorely wanted to activate the mech combat suit immediately, but Sergeant Wade had repeatedly warned him to wait until he was outside the plane. He suddenly realized that he hadn't had a chance to empty his jacket pockets. He had been planning to prank Mason with "Hard-As-Air", a small can of ... *something* he had nicked from the Inventory; a quick read of the label made it sound like the kind of fun that would annoy his friend.

"Wait," he said, trying to rummage with his free hand. "I have—"

"This is it! Coming to a stop!" yelled Wade from the cramped cockpit.

Everybody jerked as the Eiodolon came to a sudden stop, the aircraft's inertia dampers kicking in to stop them from splattering against the hull. Dev was still trying to remember the simulation, so he wasn't expecting Lot to push him towards the ramp.

"Go! Go!" she hollered.

Dev turned his head and caught her expression of delight, quickly followed by Mason giving him a weak thumbs up. Followed by a firm kick to the bum.

Dev stumbled down the tail ramp. Tripped, but didn't hit the ground ... at least, not yet. That was because they were hovering a hundred storeys above Toronto's busy streets.

The wind was deafening as Dev fell to earth. He felt a wave of panic overcome him: would his combat suit protect him, or would he splatter against the ground? Then more irrational thoughts crept in: would the Hard-As-Air can burst with the change in air pressure and blow his leg off? Would he have a chance to finish his maths homework?

His brain was desperately trying to distract Dev from the real fear: heights.

Free-falling certainly wasn't this terrifying in the combat simulations he'd practised back in the Inventory, where the worst thing that could happen was him "dying", then removing his helmet and going off to school. There was no simulation for the terror now coursing through his body, or the intensifying feeling of butterflies in his stomach. Or should that be wasps? It felt horrid enough.

Dev's fingers bunched into a fist, and he had just enough presence of mind to focus his unique form of synaesthesia — a power he possessed that allowed him to control machinery. The Iron Fist gauntlet didn't let him down. Within seconds a rush of expanding hexagonal plates covered his body, cocooning him in the comfortable exo-armour and completely sealing off the roar of the wind.

The helmet illuminated with a complete view of the outside world, as if his head were in a glass bubble. The scene was overlaid with information that was projected straight into his eyeballs, corresponding to his fixed range of vision, so he could see all the data wherever he looked.

Such as the altimeter's reading, which was rapidly descending.

It was at that point that Dev sighed, wishing that the World Consortium had developed the mech suit further. Twisting wildly as he plummeted towards earth, he thought it was a real shame that the Iron Fist couldn't fly. Nor did it have a workable parachute.

Margery Steinbeck knew that today was going to be an unusual day. It began with a vivid dream in which her recently deceased budgie had told her the winning lottery numbers. She went to the shop to buy her lottery ticket, and on her way there a futuristic dart-shaped aircraft suddenly appeared overhead with a thunderous boom. That was swiftly followed by the unexpected alarm bell of the bank she was passing. The weirdness escalated when a four-and-a-half-metre-tall robot fell from the sky and landed face down in the road with such force it formed a crater.

She waited, but the robot didn't move.

It was lucky that she had stopped to watch the spectacle; otherwise she would have been flattened by three cartoon characters barrelling from the bank – a frog, a moose and a duck. The trio of masked figures were carrying large bags, and they stopped short when they saw the giant robot lying face down in the street. Then they turned their heads simultaneously and saw five police cars skidding around the corner, sirens screaming.

That was when Margery noticed that the thieves appeared to be wearing jetpacks. Flames shot from the packs and the bank robbers were propelled into the air and along the street, limbs flailing, and with the occasional flurry of banknotes dropping from their bags.

Margery wondered why her budgie hadn't mentioned any of that. Still, she hurried to the shop, thinking it was all a good omen to try those lottery numbers.

Dev groaned. Not that the impact hurt him; the suit's remarkable outer shell had absorbed the impact, but it had still jarred him inside.

"Devon, you're wasting time." The voice was that of Uncle Parker, transmitted from the bunker back in the Inventory. As usual it carried with it tones of both impatience and disappointment.

"That wasn't supposed to happen," said Dev as he checked all systems were still working. He was supposed to have landed on his feet, action-hero style, but that was more difficult than it looked.

"One needs to improvise. Especially as your targets are getting away. So less self-pity, and get on your feet."

With a further grumble, Dev stood up. All he had to do was move normally and the suit obeyed. He drew himself to his full height—

And felt something slam into him from behind. A missile strike?

As he stumbled, three police cars veered sharply around him. Dev realized the fourth must have collided straight into him. That was confirmed a fraction of a second later when the car corkscrewed over his head, using his back as a ramp.

On instinct, Dev plucked the car out of the air to keep it from crashing and injuring the two policemen inside. He could see their shocked faces as he gently lowered the car back on its wheels.

"There you go, fellas."

The moment Dev released the car, the still-spinning tyres screamed and the car accelerated straight through a clothing-store window. Dev hadn't appreciated that the shocked driver hadn't had the chance to remove his foot from the accelerator pedal.

Dev could hear his uncle sigh over the radio. "Devon, please stop playing with the police and get after the thieves."

Dev bounded over the second police car that had stopped to gawp at the giant robot, and sprinted after the other two vehicles pursuing the jetpacks.

The Iron Fist mech suit's powerful strides allowed Dev to get back into the chase with just a few dozen bounds. Ahead, his targeting computer highlighted the three fleeing jetpack thieves, who were keeping low to the ground, evidently unused to flying the packs.

Meanwhile, the Inventory's computer matched the jetpacks to three prototypes that had been stolen by the Collector. The Inventory was a massive underground warehouse where the World Consortium had been hiding the world's greatest inventions for centuries. Dev and his uncle had been tasked to look after the collection until ... it had all gone spectacularly wrong.

"OK, Devon, this should be easy. I suggest you use the mech's magnetic impulse."

The Iron Fist was a high-tech shell originally designed by wild inventor Nikola Tesla, but before it had reached its full potential, the suit had been mothballed and stored in the Inventory. The Collector hadn't managed to pilfer the suit in his raid on the Inventory, so Consortium scientists had studied it and added a few modifications. Dev didn't need to push switches or talk; he simply used his special ability to feel his way through the computer system, which looked, in his mind's eye, like a labyrinth of glowing corridors, musical tones and pulsing lights – all a side effect of his synaesthesia.

Dev activated the MagImpulse and saw the hexagonal plates on his forearm bulge as the material reconfigured itself into the weapon. He aimed at the closest thief, the frog, and fired.

There was no bang, no flash of light. Nothing visible at all. An invisible magnetic pulse struck the jetpack, and the thief was yanked backwards as if a bungee cord were attached to him, stolen hundred-dollar banknotes spewing from his bag. Dev caught him and ripped the jetpack from the man's back. The thief dropped, landing on the bonnet of a police car below.

Dev was surprised how easy it was. "That's one." He attached the jetpack to a clip on his back and sprinted after the remaining two robbers as they sharply banked down another street of towering skyscrapers.

"Devon?"

"I know, I know," Dev snapped back. His uncle was

watching his every move as it was relayed by a satellite miles above his head.

Dev quickened his pace as the second jetpacker came into view. The thief, still wearing his Mega-Moose mask, flipped on to his back as easily as if he were swimming through water and raised a gun. Dev wasn't too concerned; he knew from experience that the Iron Fist suit was bulletproof.

Charles Parker's warning came again. "Devon!"

"I see it!" Dev snapped back. "Please stop talking and let me do this."

The man fired, and Dev made no attempt to avoid the shot, expecting it to ricochet off him.

But it was no bullet.

A glob of plasma stuck to the side of Dev's suit, and he felt a surge of electricity ripple through the mech with such intensity that he heard a flood of voices. His veins felt as if they were on fire – and he blacked out.

THRILL
SEEKER

A harsh chorus of alarms roused Dev back to consciousness. It took a moment for him to assess the situation. He was still encased in the suit, but he was lying in the middle of the road. The plasma blast had somehow short-circuited the mech, and he had stumbled backwards ... and had tripped over a postal truck, judging by the envelopes blowing around him.

Charles Parker's voice came over the audio: "Devon, you need—"

Dev had no desire for a lecture, so he muted both the incoming transmission and the irritating alarms. The moose-masked thief who'd shot him was now doubling back, eager to see the results of his handiwork. Dev guessed that the weapon was another object stolen from the Inventory. A quick check revealed that all his systems were functioning, so no real harm done.

Dev played dead, biding his time as his attacker came closer. Then he sprang. The mech moved so swiftly that the thief had no chance to react as Dev flipped to his feet in a single smooth move. At the same time, he swiped the gun from the man's hand with such force that the weapon shattered into several pieces – and probably his hand too.

The thief shot straight into the air, but Dev reached out and snagged his foot, bringing the man to a complete stop. Mega Moose howled in pain as the jetpack tried to push him upwards – but his leg stretched as if tied to a medieval rack.

"Going down," snarled Dev as he yanked the rocket pack from the man's back. The guy fell, splashing into an ornate fountain. He was no longer Dev's problem; the cops could deal with him.

Dev locked the second jetpack next to the other on his back. Almost immediately he felt the mech lift; just as he'd hoped, two rocket packs together were powerful enough to carry the suit. His uncle had explained that Dev's abilities also allowed him to make totally different gadgets communicate and work with one another, essentially reprogramming them with just a thought, meaning he was able to create new inventions on the go. It was an unexpected side effect of his condition that he was only now learning to master.

Dev looked around for the final rocketeer, Dandy Duck. He spotted the jetpack's telltale contrail curving upwards between two high-rises. With a quick mental command, Dev's rocket packs burst to life and he was suddenly soaring upwards.

The suit was not very aerodynamic, but as long as he didn't look straight down, he could handle his fear of heights . . . sort of. He could just imagine the look of delight on Lot's face if she were able to do this.

He took a corner a little too wide and scraped along the side of a tower clock, leaving a diagonal scar of broken glass and masonry.

"Sorry!" he yelled.

The jet trails looped through the sky like a roller coaster. He resisted the urge to pull a loop-the-loop; he wasn't confident that he wouldn't crash, and he had no desire to throw up in the mech's cramped interior.

Dev didn't have to follow the trail to see where the remaining thief was. Ahead was the CN Tower, a slender needle of concrete and steel that had a UFO-like observation deck three-quarters of the way up. It was the highest point in the city, and the thief stood on the edge of the uppermost observation deck. He was holding a trembling woman in his arms.

She wore a bright orange boiler suit. Dev was puzzled as to how the woman had got there in the first place; he knew the jetpacks didn't have the lift capability to carry her from the ground. Then he noticed several other figures a few metres further down the observation deck, dressed in similar orange suits, and he understood. The CN Tower allowed thrill seekers to walk around the outer edge, tethered by a single cable. The thief must have snatched her from the group as a hostage.

Dev orbited the tower, unsure what to do. He could blast Dandy Duck off the tower, but he was pretty sure the thief would take the woman with him. She might be a thrill seeker, but free-falling without a parachute was probably not something she'd had in mind.

He landed on the roof, several metres away from

them. When Dev spoke, the mech amplified his voice in harsh, aggressive tones. "Let the woman go!"

"I will, man!" The thief's voice wavered. "Straight off the edge. Four hundred and fifty metres straight down! You want that on your conscience, man? 'Cause I'll do it!" To emphasize his point, he pushed the woman closer to the edge. It was a small gesture, but enough for her to shriek in terror.

Dev's blood ran cold. He was no hostage negotiator, and now a person's life was in his hands. Behind them he could see the Eiodolon hovering at a discreet distance over the vast expanse of Lake Ontario.

Even though he had superior strength and several weapons at his disposal, Dev was out of options. He only had one weapon left – the truth.

The thief watched, astonished, as the tiles forming the mech suit partially peeled away, revealing Dev standing inside. The sight of a fourteen-year-old boy shocked both the adults.

The thief peeled his Dandy Duck mask off and renewed his grip on the woman. "Is this a joke?"

Dev jumped down from the suit and held his hands up to show he was unarmed. He tried to ignore the strong wind that could easily blow him over the edge.

His legs trembled at the mere thought of how high they were. "No joke. It's just me. So you really don't need a hostage, do you? I mean, against a *kid*?"

The thief looked frantically around, expecting a surprise attack – but there was nobody else.

"You've got a bag of money" – Dev pointed to the bag in the man's free hand – "and a rocket pack. I'd say that's all you need for a really good time. You don't need to hurt anybody."

The thief squinted in thought, and he glanced sidelong at his hostage with a look of regret. "I reckon you've got a point, kid. Things get out of control real fast. I didn't want anyone gettin' hurt." He nodded at the mech. "Where d'you get that thing?"

"It's from the same place as your rocket pack."

The man's brow knitted into a frown.

Dev realized that the man didn't know where the packs were from. "So ... did someone give that pack to you?"

Dev was surprised to see the bafflement on the man's face as he tried to remember. He looked at the bag of money as if for the first time. "I don't—"

The man suddenly dropped to his knees, releasing the woman and the bag of money, and clutched his head. He howled in pain.

The woman started to run towards Dev.

Then several things happened at once.

The man's eyes were wide, his face pulled in a rictus of agony as he yelled through gritted teeth. "Leave me alone!"

A gust of wind blew the bag over, the money erupting from it in a cloud of banknotes that blinded the woman. The next thing Dev knew, she had tumbled to the floor, and both the man and the woman were rolling towards the edge.

"NO!" Dev lunged for them – remembering too late that he was *out* of the mech suit, and had no jetpack to save his life.

Both the thief and woman rolled over the edge with a screech. And Dev couldn't stop himself from following. . .

In the cockpit of the Eiodolon, Sergeant Wade squinted as she watched the distant figures. She wished the craft had been fitted with surveillance cameras, as had originally been intended, but as it was just a prototype that had been consigned to the shelves of the Inventory, nobody had bothered. She hadn't dared get too close, worrying that the aircraft's presence would spook the thief.

"What the heck is he doing?"

The cockpit was just big enough for a pilot, so Lot was forced to peer over Wade's shoulder. She had a headset on and had been repeatedly trying to contact Dev.

"He's out of the suit! No wonder he's not answering the radio!"

Mason shoved his head through the narrow gap over Wade's other shoulder. "Wow! Look at that! If he's not careful he'll fall. No, wait . . . he's fallen."

Wade's left hand was already pulling the throttle backwards with such force that both Lot and Mason were thrown to the back of the craft before the inertia dampers were able to kick in. Wade wasn't exactly sure *what* she could do to save all three of them, so she prayed that a solution would present itself in the next twenty seconds, before they had a rather gory meeting with the ground.

It was at times like this that Dev was glad he didn't listen to his uncle's boring rules. Especially about not taking things out of the Inventory without authorization. Not that there was a massive amount left on the shelves since the break-in, but what there was could still be useful, in the right situation. He hoped this was one such case.

Even as his feet cartwheeled over his head and, for the third time that day, his stomach lurched, Dev's fingers closed over the small can in his jacket pocket.

As he dropped he could hear nothing but the wind screaming against his ears. With both hands he pointed the Hard-As-Air can towards the ground and thumbed the button on top.

Here goes nothing, he thought.

The can gave a slight vibration as the pavement swept up to meet them. The air around him felt increasingly thick, as if he was now travelling through water, then feathers. Just metres from the ground the three of them came to a gentle stop as the air beneath them became so dense it was like falling into a duvet. Breathing became impossible for a few moments, the air like gulping thick soup, but soon the density dissipated.

The woman gasped for breath, then looked around in astonishment, then burst into tears of relief. The thief was unconscious, having fainted from fear.

A shadow covered them all as the Eiodolon approached. Dev smiled, feeling quite pleased with himself. All things considered, for a first mission, he would rate it a success.

Although he'd had it with heights. No matter what the next mission was, he was going to keep his feet firmly on the ground, just where gravity wanted them to be.

COMPLAINT PROCEDURE

"That was a complete disaster!" said Charles Parker as he paced the Inventory canteen.

A few World Consortium technicians sat at far tables, assiduously minding their own business. Dev remembered when the underground rooms and corridors of the Inventory used to be empty, just home to him, his uncle and the spherical automated defence robot called Eema. He had the run of the place, but since the heist the World Consortium had all but moved in. The corridors and warehouses teemed with serious people everywhere, all performing very serious tasks very seriously as they reorganized the remaining artefacts and worked with Charles Parker to track down the many missing ones.

"We got all three rocket packs back," Dev pointed out. "Mission accomplished!"

"And he didn't destroy that much," Mason added — but quickly fell silent under Charles's icy gaze. Charles may have been Dev's uncle, but he was also Mason's boss.

Lot was sitting on a table next to Mason, her feet swinging, and behind them stood Sergeant Wade, who avoided looking Charles in the eye.

Charles pointed to Mason, Lot and Sergeant Wade. "You three, fine. There was little you could have done. But you, Dev... This was supposed to be a stealth mission. And you never, ever leave the Iron Fist suit. What if he had stolen that?"

Dev shrugged. "He wouldn't have been able to use it."

"That's not a chance I am willing to take. You destroyed several vehicles, took a chunk out of a building, and almost got an innocent bystander killed! We're supposed to be a *secret* organization!"

Dev's anger rose. "Well, that's easy for you to say, you weren't even there! You just watched everything from here, making unhelpful comments!"

"At least the DigiJam worked," Wade cut in, hoping to ease the tension.

Charles nodded, a thin smile of pride pulling at his cheeks. Using the digital jammer had been his idea. It prevented any cameras in the area from recording, so there would be no video footage of the mech suit, rocket packs or advanced fighter jets, and, as usual, tales of such things would become urban myths circulating the internet that are soon forgotten.

"Lucky for us it did," Charles said.

"So, mission accomplished," said Dev, standing up and stretching.

His uncle raised an eyebrow. "Where do you think you're going?"

Dev motioned towards Lot and Mason. "We're getting out of here and finding something fun to do."

His uncle gave a humourless laugh. "Of course you are. Although I fear you may have got a little mixed up with all the travelling." He tapped his watch. "It's now morning, which means you better hurry or you'll be late for school."

"School?" Mason spat the word out. Watching Dev all day had been tiring work, and he'd been looking forward to doing nothing more than returning home and sleeping.

"We need to keep up appearances," said Wade. "Plus your education is important. Dismissed."

They filed out of the room, but before Dev exited, his uncle stopped him, placing a hand on his shoulder and turning him around. His other hand was extended.

With a sigh, Dev handed over the Hard-As-Air can.

"What have I told you about taking things from the Inventory?"

"I was just messing with it," Dev mumbled.

Charles shook his head, rubbing his tired eyes. Dev thought he looked far older than the fifty-something he was and suspected the stress of the job was getting to him. Charles held the can up. "How many times do I need to say this: until we know where the rest of the inventions are, and what the Collector had planned to do with them, we can't afford to take any chances."

Dev nodded. He didn't look him in the eye, though. He didn't trust him. Dev was still angry about learning he hadn't actually been born; he had been artificially created, to guard the Inventory. A task his "uncle" was continually pointing out that he'd failed at.

Dev turned and quickly left the room. Even school would be better than spending another minute with Charles Parker.

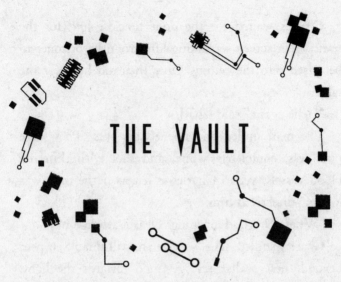

THE VAULT

The light was a special kind of light. The bulb gave a constant high-pitched trill that grated the patience of anybody unfortunate enough to have to sit at the table for too long.

Right now there was only one person seated there. One hand lay over the other, and his eyes were closed. He ignored the headache throbbing in his temples. He wore a one-piece blue prison uniform, and his hair was shaved so short that a network of scars across his scalp was visible.

He didn't react as the only door to the circular room hissed open and Charles Parker entered.

Charles waited for the door to close and for the transparent screen separating him from the prisoner to be raised into the ceiling. Only then did he sit at the table.

"Hello again," said Charles.

The man smiled and opened his eyes. They were pupil-less, completely white, and shot with thin red blood vessels, yet to Charles it felt as if the man was looking directly at him.

"What? No good morning? Or is it afternoon?"

Charles smiled. "Ah, so you are still unable to peer beyond these walls?" He gestured towards the light. "That's because of the lights we have developed. They work on a very specific wavelength that ensures you can't see too far."

The prisoner, known only as the Collector, leaned back in his chair. His special vision usually allowed him to see through the whole spectrum of light – from X-rays to ultraviolet. It would give him an advantage if he could see through the walls of his prison and work out exactly where he was being held. The lights here only allowed him to see a distance of three metres; anything further was just a black void.

The Collector tilted his head. "Coming here to gloat

is not your usual style, *father*." He let the last word drag out, dripping with venom. For, like Dev, the Collector was not born but artificially created in a laboratory. Although he looked to be in his thirties, his real age was far younger. The project had been one of many developed by the World Consortium to push the limits of science into new areas – including unethical ones.

Charles was unperturbed. He'd heard it all before, having endured for years a daily barrage of insults from Dev.

"Helix," said Charles.

"Shadow Helix is the name of the organization that employed my services. I have told you this on several occasions. They paid me. They supplied the people and equipment, and I carried out the work."

"But that's not entirely true, is it?"

The Collector's face remained expressionless.

Charles leaned across the desk. "I know you were Double Helix's right-hand man. I know he trusted you."

The Collector smiled. "If he trusted me as you say, then why would I tell you anything about him?"

"Indeed." Charles sat back, his eyes fixed on the prisoner. "OK, then, let's talk about you. The Collector. Quite a fitting name: you did well *collecting* a huge number of our . . . *items* and extracting them before being caught yourself."

The Collector shrugged. "I tried my best."

"I had assumed that your new stolen 'collection' would stay together. I would have thought Double Helix would want all that technology for his own personal use."

The Collector remained silent.

Charles propped both elbows on the table and leaned forward. "So I find it somewhat baffling that some items have shown up in various locations around the world, in the hands of petty criminals. Some of your men, Lee and the others, still remain at large. Yet what they took seems to appear in the most surprising of places."

The Collector sighed dramatically and said, "Those items probably just . . . slipped through the cracks. My men can be so absent-minded."

"Not that absent-minded. Those items have been deliberately handed over. I just fail to see why. And Double Helix never does anything without a plan."

"Ordinarily I would agree with you. However, if he has such ideas, then he didn't share them with me. In fact, I must not be as valuable to him as you say. If that were true, I would have hoped he would try to get me out of here. Yet here I am."

Silence gripped the room as Charles tensed. For a moment he half expected the walls to explode and the Collector to be rescued . . . but nothing happened.

The Collector sighed again. "Alas, I am not any wiser to Double Helix's plans." A thoughtful look passed across his face. "Perhaps if you were to give me the details of where and with whom you have found the Inventory stock, I could assist you?"

Charles was surprised. "You would work *against* your boss?"

"Since it doesn't look as if he's ready to charge in here and rescue his old friend, then I suppose I don't owe him any loyalty." He treated Charles to a smile.

The sort of smile that belonged to a shark before it was about to strike.

JUST
ANOTHER DAY

It was rather surprising how things could change in such a short time. Dev used to hate school. The lessons were boring, and he used to be bullied mercilessly – especially by one particular kid, who did his best to publicly humiliate Dev at every opportunity. As a result, Dev avoided interacting with his fellow pupils at all costs.

But now, due to recent events, school wasn't so bad. The lessons were still boring, of course, but at least Dev's constant run-ins with his bully had vanished. That's because the bully had been Mason, Dev's new partner in crime.

When the Collector raided the inventory, they were

forced to work together, and they became friends ...
of a sort. The kind of friends who didn't acknowledge
each other's existence in public. The sort of friends
who didn't really like each other and had nothing in
common, yet when it came to crunch time they could
depend on each other with their lives.

That suited Dev perfectly. It kept Mason and his
thuggish pals at arm's length; Mason now spent most of
his spare time playing rugby. The other students didn't
know what to think, so they gave Dev an even wider
berth.

The situation with Lot, on the other hand, was
a disappointment. Dev really wanted to spend more
time with her, but she had completely embraced the
concept of a secret society and refused to do anything
to jeopardize that. She kept herself active with her usual
school friends, and he only saw a blur of blonde hair race
past or caught her infectious smile across the playground
before she quickly turned away and ignored him.

So Dev's days became a stream of trying to pretend
his teachers weren't going too slowly through the
curriculum, followed by lonely walks through the sleepy
town of Edderton, back to the place he reluctantly called
home – a farm that was a surface decoy, concealing

a sprawling complex of warehouses and corridors far below the ground.

The farm had been a smouldering ruin by the time the Collector had finished with it, but the World Consortium had quickly rebuilt it exactly as before, and a gas explosion had been blamed for the noises and devastation heard across the town.

While enduring another physics lesson with Mr Morgan, Dev let his mind wander. The talk of Isaac Newton being amazed as an apple fell on him failed to thrill Dev, and he found the maths behind the second law of motion – *resultant force (N) = mass (kg) × acceleration (m/s²)* – easy to solve. His uncle had told him that another by-product of his synaesthesia was skill with mathematics. So instead Dev began to dwell on the problem that had been consuming him for weeks: instead of being born like everybody else around him, Dev had been engineered into existence. Made. In the heart of the Inventory's most secure Red Zone, Dev had discovered the lab he'd been grown in. He'd been designed with special abilities to be a living key to protect the Inventory's contents. His code name had been Iron Fist, a name he'd now assigned to his battle armour.

That meant Dev had no parents. Technically he wasn't even an orphan. Charles Parker was the closest thing he had to family, but Uncle Parker was not really an uncle, more like Dev's creator.

Dev now didn't consider himself to be an actual *person*, although Charles had taken great pains to assure him that he was. Dev was as human as the next kid in school.

But with extras.

He had been manufactured to replace the Collector, a failed prototype. Did that make the villain his brother?

Several times he had asked Charles Parker to allow him to visit the Collector, and each time Dev had been refused. No longer willing to take his uncle's decisions as final, he had turned to Sergeant Wade, who represented the Consortium that ran the Inventory. Disappointingly, she always referred Dev back to his uncle, pointing out that – however vague the family connection – Charles Parker was still his legal guardian.

Mr Morgan's voice broke into his musings. "Mr Parker? Earth to Mr Parker?" Dev sat up and tried to look interested. "Could you please enlighten us as to what Newton's laws of motion are."

Dev hadn't been listening, but he knew this. It was just that his memory refused to call up the information.

Mr Morgan crossed his arms, his eyes almost concealed by his fluffy caterpillar-like eyebrows as he frowned. "I'm waiting."

"Um, stop, drop and roll?" said Dev desperately. The class burst into tittering laughter, and he felt his cheeks burn with embarrassment.

"Impressive, Devon. Well, you can learn them in detention tonight."

Dev was no stranger to detention. In fact, he often relished it as an excuse not to go home. This evening, however, he didn't want to be there. He had hoped to catch Lot on the way home so he could talk through the concerns bothering him. She was the only one who would listen and understand what he was going through.

Dev spent thirty minutes reading a rather dry textbook about Sir Isaac Newton's contributions to science while his teacher sat at the front of the class marking homework. After looking forlornly at his coffee cup, Mr Morgan excused himself.

Dev flipped the page and stared at the bland text: *for every action there is an equal and opposite reaction.* Dev yawned.

"Hello, Dev."

Dev looked up. There was nobody in the room. He checked his phone and watch, in case they had activated without him knowing, but they were both on silent mode. Had he imagined the whisper?

"I know you can hear me."

The voice sounded as if the speaker was directly next to his ear. Dev bolted to his feet so sharply that he knocked his chair over. He slashed his arm through the air behind him, just in case the speaker was invisible. Still nobody.

"Where are you?" said Dev, his eyes darting across the classroom for any signs of movement.

"That's not really the question you should be asking, is it?"

That's all Dev needed right now, a smart-mouthed ghost. His eyes fell on his water bottle; he could have sworn he'd seen movement there.

"OK, then: *who* are you?"

A gentle mocking laughter floated around the room. As Dev watched, concentric circles vibrated across the surface of the water in his bottle.

"Bravo. That is the correct question."

Dev gently touched the table as the stranger spoke. He could feel the vibrations through the plastic-coated wood and saw ripples form across the surface of his water bottle. Was the voice somehow projecting in the room and resonating off everything?

The voice continued. "I am somebody who is looking out for you, Dev."

"That's kind of you," said Dev as he rushed to the window to see if anybody was outside, somehow projecting the voice through the window. But the yard beyond was empty. "But I prefer my friends, you know, a little more visible."

"You have a greater purpose than being a puppet for Charles Parker, and I intend to help you achieve that."

"What if I just want to be left alone?"

"I know you better than you think. I want to help you. To warn you: never believe your eyes. There is more happening around you than you realize. We shall meet soon enough."

"Who are you?"

There was no answer. Dev turned around and saw Mr Morgan had re-entered the room with a steaming cup of coffee. One hand was still on the door handle. His expression was one of bemusement.

"Um ... it's me. Are you feeling OK, Devon?" His eyes moved to Dev's toppled chair.

Dev felt a flush of embarrassment and hurried to right the chair. "Just thinking of drama class. Practising a scene from. . ." He didn't know how to finish the sentence, so he lapsed into silence.

"This is detention, not some sort of rehearsal space. Your time's up, though, so you can go do that someplace else now. And, uh, break a leg."

Dev smiled weakly at Mr Morgan, nodded, gathered his things and hurried from the classroom before he started hearing any more disembodied voices.

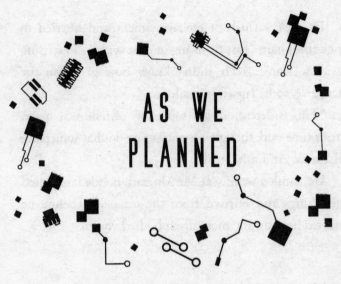

AS WE PLANNED

Mason yawned as the giant screen in front of him changed to depict a map of the world. He was in the Inventory command bunker, so this was no normal screen, but a holographic one; the globe gently rotated in three dimensions. Lot nudged him in the ribs.

"What?" Mason said quietly. "I didn't get much sleep before they woke me up for this."

Charles Parker used his hand to rotate the map so all three teens could see Asia. He moved his fingers apart to zoom in on a long island at the edge of the Pacific Ocean.

"Japan. More specifically, Tokyo. The World

Consortium has picked up reports that a piece of Inventory technology has found its way there."

"So it's something small?" said Dev with a frown. Some of the missing equipment was so huge and cumbersome that it was hard to imagine it going anywhere without drawing attention. "That will make it harder to find."

"Not necessarily. We don't know which item it is." Charles pointed to another screen. Surveillance pictures appeared of a powerful-looking man climbing out of a car. "This is Christen Sandberg, a South African crime lord with a vicious rap sheet. He was previously spotted in America, and now he's just arrived in Japan."

"So you think he has something to do with the Inventory loot?" asked Lot.

"We don't know for sure."

"Great. So is there anything you do know?" said Lot brightly. She met Charles's gaze, refusing to look away first.

"That is why you are going there to track him down, and hopefully he will lead you to the missing item. Then you will retrieve the gadget with, and I can't stress this enough, the *minimum of fuss*. So, to that aim, you are leaving the mech suit here." He deactivated the screens. "Your last mission left way too much collateral damage, and we can't risk a repeat of that in a city as densely populated as Tokyo."

Dev looked at his two companions with a puzzled frown.

"Is that it?"

Charles Parker didn't look up as he busied himself on a computer. "Yes. Eema will see you to your transport."

With a soft rumble, a large metal sphere rolled up to the door. As it stopped, metallic spike-like legs emerged from the body to stabilize it. A holographic head appeared, displaying a bright yellow smiley emoji. This was Eema, the Inventory's artificially intelligent security system.

"Follow me," she said.

Her legs retracted and she rolled down the corridor with Dev, Lot and Mason following behind.

Dev couldn't hide his surprise. They may have only been on one real mission, but his uncle had dragged them through countless long briefings on how they were to behave during missions, and none had been so short. Furthermore, Sergeant Wade had always been with them, but now there was no sign of her, and he couldn't imagine that she had anything more important to do than attend a mission briefing.

A handful of scientists passed them, hunched over their tablets as they discussed their research.

"Eema, where are we going?" Dev finally asked.

"To the hangar." Ever since the break-in, a small special area had been reworked to allow quick and easy access from the Inventory, but under the most stringent security procedures. "Your aircraft is being prepared for you there."

They walked the rest of the way in silence. The hangar was a hive of activity. Several technicians removed hoses and electrical wires from the undercarriage of a large aircraft that was mostly hidden behind a canvas sheet. Dev could see the excitement on Lot and Mason's faces, and he was reminded how new this was to them still. They hadn't yet tired of discovering the contents of the Inventory, even though most of it was missing.

"Where's Sergeant Wade?"

"Your new ride does not require Sergeant Wade to pilot it." Eema led the way to the aircraft. "Unless you feel you are unable to conduct the mission on your own? If you need a babysitter . . ."

"No way!" snapped Mason. "We're totally ready."

Dev didn't reply. He knew Eema was more than a machine. She was capable of just as much subtlety and sarcasm as he was, and she was definitely trying to provoke a reaction from them. But he wasn't sure why. It was as if they were being tested.

"Here's your ride," said Eema with a wink. "It's rather cool."

"Robots can't pull off saying 'cool'," said Dev gruffly.

Eema's mechanical arm unfurled from her body and pulled the canvas away.

"No way!" said Lot, her mouth hanging open in astonishment.

Dev tried to conceal a sudden thrill of excitement. For several years he had walked past an odd shape hidden under a canvas sheet, tucked in the corner of the Inventory. He had often wondered what it was, but now he knew.

It was an olive-green disc about ten metres in diameter, in the classic flying saucer shape, with hemisphere on top and a bowl-shaped hull below. It rested on five stubby legs, and a ramp lowered from the underbelly led inside. On closer examination, Dev couldn't see any lines across the hull, as if it was made from a single piece. Running from the central canopy to the rim, on opposite sides, was a sunken access ladder on which a technician was perched, examining something.

"Is that a real. . .?" Mason began.

Eema's emoji face winked, pulling a virtual tongue. It was a little disconcerting to see a robot do that. "We just call it the Avro. It's the descendant of the United States Air Force's VZ-9 Avrocar, built in Nevada, USA. It has a silent negative-grav drive, total cloaking ability, and this is where we originally obtained the DigiJam tech. It will take you halfway around the planet before you notice, and you don't have to lift a finger. Your flight is preprogrammed."

"Awesome!" said Mason, running his hand across the hull.

Dev noticed a look of disappointment cross Lot's face. She liked to play around with the tech, control it — not sit there and do nothing.

"So that's it? We don't actually do anything?"

Eema gestured towards the ramp. "All aboard. I've packed a kitbag of useful gadgets for the mission. Don't draw attention to either yourself or the technology. Remember your training, and stick to the plan."

The short walk up the ramp led them to the cockpit, the only room on board. Dev thought the interior of the craft felt more like a home theatre, with three leather chairs in the middle of the circular cockpit facing a wrap-around window that took up half the front wall. There was a crescent-shaped, angled panel below the window, presumably a control panel, but it was smooth and featureless. Kitbags had been left on each of the seats. He didn't recall seeing a window on the outside, so he reasoned that it was some kind of one-way screen.

Dev patted the back of one of the three seats. "I guess that explains why Wade isn't coming with us."

"I'm surprised they're letting us do this on our own, after all the complaints last time," said Lot, taking the middle seat. She rummaged through the kitbag. She pulled out a pair of shades and three silver pin badges; there was no explanation as to their purpose. She dropped them inside with a frown and extracted a blue plastic cylinder. The label, in groovy 1960s font, read: *SHOK-BALLS!*[TM] The jagged lines coming from the illustration indicated the contents were charged with electricity.

She threw it back and found what looked like a fat thermos flask. She read the label. "EverFrost – *keeps your drinks cold for ever!*" She opened it – and a smoky wisp of gas seeped out. "Wow! That's cold! How does it get your drink so chilled without freezing it? And for ever? Weird."

Mason checked his own bag and pulled out a golf-ball-sized object. The two separate hemispheres turned in opposite directions, but it didn't seem to do anything else. He saw a logo on the side, the name written in a circle around it: AttentionGrabber. "I don't get it. What's this supposed to do?" He tossed the AttentionGrabber back in the bag. "All of this stuff looks rubbish! What was Eema thinking?"

Dev took his seat. He still couldn't shake the feeling that they were being tested, or worse, that his uncle really had no idea what was waiting for them.

The blank, smooth surface of the panel below the window suddenly bubbled and transformed, with buttons and screens appearing from nowhere.

Lot traced her fingers over them. "Incredible. It's like liquid metal." She noticed a set of controls had appeared in front of her, and they were not dissimilar to a helicopter's cyclic, collective and pedals. She experimentally pulled at them, but nothing happened. She poked some of the buttons. "There must be a manual override here somewhere. . ."

"Stop pressing stuff," said Mason. "Eema said it was all preprogrammed."

The entrance ramp folded up behind them,

seamlessly merging with the wall. Lot quickly raised her hands off the controls.

"I didn't touch anything!"

According to the screen, they were already lifting up through the hangar.

"Wow," said Mason. "I can't feel a thing!"

They passed through the Inventory's roof doors, which swiftly opened as they approached. The section of floor in front of them suddenly became translucent, so they could see directly below as the roof slid closed, camouflaged with crops. In seconds they passed through clouds, but there was still no sense of movement inside the vehicle.

Lot pulled a face. "Yeah, so much for excitement." She slumped back in her seat, arms folded.

Dev smiled. Every time they had flown, Lot had got excited whenever they had hit turbulence. If this was going to be a smooth, long ride, then she was going to be in a bad mood when they arrived.

Just over an hour had passed when Eema's voice chimed around the cockpit, surprising them all. "Prepare for arrival."

TOKYO CALLING

In the night-time, crazy, multicoloured, neon noise of the Shinjuku ward of Tokyo, it was unlikely anybody would notice the appearance of a flying saucer. But not even the keenest observer would have had the chance, as the Avro's cloaking device made it appear like nothing more than a shimmering haze in the air when it landed in the quiet, fenced-off Gyoen National Garden.

Dev slung the kitbag over his shoulder as he led Lot and Mason down the ramp. To anybody watching, it would have looked like they'd stepped out of thin air. Dev scanned the dark park, while Lot had her nose in her Inventory-issue mobile phone.

"So thirteen-and-a-half million people live here," said Lot with an exasperated sigh, "and we're supposed to find one specific guy?"

"How hard can it be," said Mason flippantly.

"Uh, guys, we have company!" said Dev as a uniformed guard ran from the shadows, shouting in Japanese.

"Can either of you speak Japanese?" asked Mason.

Dev was about to make a joke back when he realized he could. They all could. He reached into his pocket and pulled out a small wireless headphone piece. He shoved it into his ear the same moment the guard shone a torch into Dev's eyes. Instinctively, Dev raised his hands to shield his eyes, with the bonus effect of covering his face.

"You are trespassing!" snapped the guard, his voice being translated from Japanese in real time. The only problem was it didn't translate Dev's own voice, so any response in English probably wouldn't be understood. "You are under arrest!"

Great, thought Dev. They'd only been here thirty seconds and already they were in trouble. His fingers moved over his watch, which was in fact quite special – the smartwatch that other smartwatches longed to be.

It communicated directly back to base and to the Avro behind them.

Colours flashed in Dev's vision and he heard pleasant digital chimes. They weren't real; they were the effects of his synaesthesia ability, audio and visual guides that allowed him to navigate the smartwatch by touch and sense alone. In a split second his watch sent the command to the aircraft's main computer.

The guard reached for his radio, intent on reporting the intruders. He had raised it to his mouth when Dev deactivated the aircraft's cloaking device – and the Avro materialized behind them. The guard's mouth dropped open in astonishment.

Mason raised his hand and pulled his face in the most grotesque gurn he could. Then he croaked in the most alien voice he could conjure up. "We come in peace, earthling!"

The guard keeled over backwards, having passed out from the shock of his close encounter.

"We come in peace?" Dev laughed as they hurried down the street. He still had tears streaming down his cheeks.

"Always wanted to say that," grinned Mason.

They had spent ten minutes dragging the guard

back to his little security booth and propping him in his chair. They hoped that when he woke, he'd assume it had all been a dream. The ship was invisible once again, now hovering out of human reach, and any surveillance cameras in the area would have automatically been "mysteriously" blanked by the aircraft's stealth technology.

Lot used the map on her phone to guide them down a network of streets, and the buildings around them became taller, illuminated with signs and brand names. The streets themselves became increasingly busy and loud as the roads widened and the traffic increased. With so many people around, nobody questioned three young teenagers strolling late at night.

Lot glanced up from her phone. "According to the intel report, this Christen person should be staying in that hotel." They all looked up at the sleek tower rising before them. Dev let out a low whistle.

"That's got to be fifty or sixty stories tall." The promise to himself about avoiding heights was proving more difficult than he had hoped. "So if the stolen item is in there, do we just walk in and get it, or do we wait for this Christen to leave and follow him – hopefully to the item itself?"

Lot and Mason exchanged a look, then shrugged. They hadn't been given a plan during the briefing, and the flight had been so short – ultrasonic, according to Eema – that they'd arrived before thinking to discuss the next steps.

"I think we need to ask some questions," said Dev, pressing the phone option on his smartwatch. In seconds he had opened an encrypted secure communications channel to the Inventory command bunker. "Well, uncle, we arrived in one piece. Now what?"

Silence. Dev wondered if he hadn't programmed the channel correctly. "Uncle Parker?"

Eema's voice cut in. "Your uncle isn't here at the moment, Dev."

Dev felt uneasy. "Where'd he go? Don't tell me he's gone to the toilet the one time we need his help."

"He has left the Inventory for a while."

Dev could see the concern on his friends' faces. This was highly irregular. "What about Sergeant Wade?"

"There is nobody here, Dev."

"Then who's in charge?"

There was a slightly amused tone to Eema's reply. "I suppose that would be you, Dev."

Dev had always complained about not being trusted

with the tech in the Inventory, but to actually be handed *total* responsibility for his second mission was, frankly, irresponsible.

Dev couldn't keep the panic from his voice. "What am I supposed to do?"

"Simple. Retrieve the item and return it to the Inventory. What's the problem?"

Dev considered replying, but instead stabbed the disconnect button on his watch. He was fuming that Eema was proving to be so unhelpful. He looked back up at the building.

"Knowing my luck, I bet he's on the very top floor. What do you think we should do?"

Lot nudged him playfully in the arm. "Well, we've come all this way. It would be a shame if we didn't cause some trouble."

Mason nodded. "We spent all that time trying to break out of the Inventory." He nodded towards the hotel. "It's gonna be fun breaking *in* somewhere."

Despite his anger, Dev couldn't resist Lot's infectious smile. He grinned too. "Let's do this. Let's find this guy. And if he has our stuff, he won't have it for much longer."

A DARING
PLAN

The trio spent the next hour drinking milkshakes in the fast-food restaurant opposite the hotel. They dreamed up elaborate plans to determine which room Christen was staying in. Complicated diversions and risky acrobatics were considered and numerous films and books were referenced as they planned their daring break-in.

In the end, Lot had thought to ask Eema to hack into the hotel's computers, only to discover that Dev had been right all along: Christen had indeed booked the penthouse suite on the very top floor.

From there it had been a very simple process. They walked into the hotel lobby with their kitbags slung over their shoulders, smiling and acting as if they belonged there. Nobody stopped them; everyone just assumed they were guests. Dev had used his gift to trick the elevator into accepting his hand as an electronic key card, and in seconds they were in the express elevator.

Lot pouted. "That was a bit too easy."

"Yeah," said Mason. "This breaking-in lark is a lot easier than busting out of somewhere."

"Easy is good," said Dev. "Easy is our friend."

The next part of the plan was the most risky – breaking into Christen's room. They were hoping it was empty, though, as Eema had checked the hotel's key card logs and seen that he had swiped out of the room.

Again, Dev used his hand to spoof the room's key card sensor. He pushed the room door open, and they entered.

"Two visits in two days," said the Collector with a hint of a smile. "Why, Charles, you are beginning to make me think you really need me."

Charles Parker slid a thick pile of papers in between them. The Collector gave a quizzical frown.

"Paper? How unenvironmental."

"Handing you an electronic device seems a little extravagant."

The Collector was forbidden any technology for fear he would find some way to manipulate it into escaping. Instead, Sergeant Wade had spent several hours assembling and printing all the information.

"This is everything we have on Shadow Helix's latest operations," Charles said, his jaw clenching as he inhaled a deep breath to steady his nerves.

The Collector stared at the pile. His adapted eyesight allowed him to read through each layer individually, with no need to turn the pages.

Charles leaned back in his chair. "Feel free to share any insights you may have about their intentions."

"You are sending the boy to retrieve the artefacts?"

"Of course. He's on a field mission as we speak."

The Collector's head tilted up, curious. Then he continued reading. "Ah, yes. Here it is. Japan? You have sent him there?"

"To track down a fellow named Christen Sandberg. Would you happen to know how Mr Sandberg came into possession of stolen material?"

"I haven't heard of him before, although his file is quite impressive. As for how he came into possession of the artefact, he would have been selected especially. His ego, pride, lust for glory – they all make him a perfect candidate for somebody they can easily manipulate."

"For what purpose?"

"That depends on what item he was given."

Charles hesitated, then indicated to the papers. "It was an item that was not catalogued correctly."

The Collector's face lit up in delight. "Not catalogued correctly? My dear Charles, how is such a thing possible? You were always one with an attention for detail. So you don't even know what the misplaced item *is?*"

Charles's face became rigid; he refused to let the criminal see he had hit a nerve. He patted the file. "The details are in there."

The Collector's lips parted in a smile. "You have at least told Dev *who* is selecting these scapegoats for Shadow Helix?"

Charles was good at keeping his face blank. Too good. The Collector saw through his uncertainty in an instant.

"You don't know?" It was almost a gasp of astonishment. "You haven't even worked out who has taken my place at Double Helix's side while I fester in here?" The prisoner leaned across the table with a sense of urgency. "Does the name Kardach mean anything to you?"

Charles Parker hesitated. "Jim Kardach invented Bluetooth wireless technology."

The Collector stared at him. "Really? That is all you have to say? Your mind is confused by all the secrets you keep. Never once wondering if they need to be kept at all. You should warn Dev immediately. He is about to walk into a whole new world of trouble. This is when things start to turn *nasty*."

PREPARATION

"Nice," said Lot, looking around the opulent suite.

A large leather couch was positioned by an oval glass table, both of which sat before a panoramic window that filled one entire wall, offering up a twinkling sea of city lights stretching to the horizon.

Dev headed straight for the table. "Spread out. Keep an eye out for anything that looks as if it's linked to the Inventory."

Mason headed for the bedroom, and moments later Dev heard a gasp of wonder; another splendid room lay beyond. Lot headed for the open-plan kitchen and started peering in the bin.

"I hardly think he'd bin technology of the future," Dev said testily.

"I'm looking for clues. You know, ones they tried to get rid of? Or may have got wedged behind the sofa?"

Dev got the hint and dropped to the floor, peering under the couch.

Mason suddenly ran in from the bedroom, his face flushed with excitement.

"What did you find?" asked Dev.

"The toilets over here!" gasped Mason, catching his breath. "They speak to you — and even wash your bum!"

Dev blinked at him in surprise. "No way!"

Lot coughed for attention. "Uh, Dev? You live in the Inventory, with thousands of gadgets . . . and a *toilet* impresses you?"

"Our loos are broken most of the time," he said sheepishly. "Since they put in those biological ones, we've had trees growing out of them every time you take a—"

Lot slapped down a pile of shredded paper on the kitchen counter to cut him off. "Well, while you geniuses think a bog is the best thing you've ever seen, I found this."

"Scrap paper," said Mason, crossing over. "Impressive."

Lot ignored him as she straightened the papers,

revealing a mass of individual strips. "Must be something important if he took time to shred it." She carefully laid a few strips out, trying to see if they'd match to form more of the page.

"Let me," said Dev, stepping in. He took a picture of the strips with his smartwatch, and within seconds the strips on his screen had been reassembled into the correct order.

"Wow, you have an app for that?" said Lot – then corrected herself. "Of course you do. The Inventory's got everything!"

Dev shrugged. "Or, in this case, ninety-nine pence well spent from the Download Store."

The reconstructed image on Dev's screen was a map of Tokyo, with an address written at the bottom as well as a time – 22:00.

Dev glanced at his watch. "Eighteen minutes from now."

Mason toyed with the paper fragments. "That's a pretty low-tech way of keeping a secret."

Lot shook her head. "It's perfect. It can't be hacked, there are no duplicate files and, if he'd thought to burn the evidence, it can be deleted without a trace. My dad says sometimes old school ways are the best."

Dev was studying the map. "It's not far from here. We might be able to get there if we hurry."

The business district behind Shinjuku station was a nest of high-rise towers, amongst which the Mode Gakuen Cocoon Tower stood out – a futuristic marvel of white steel woven around gently curved glass walls. The streets around here were a lot quieter than those nearer the station.

The hissing brakes of a bus caught the trio's attention as it pulled up to an empty stop across the plaza. Nobody got on or off, but the driver waited patiently, maintaining his schedule.

Then a squeal of rubber made them spin around. A black van skidded around the corner and pulled up opposite them some twenty metres away. The side door slid open, and the unmistakable figure of Christen Sandberg stepped out with a case. He didn't even look around before placing it on the pavement. After unclasping the latches, he opened the case and began assembling the green plastic components inside.

Dev, Lot and Mason hadn't moved.

"He looks a lot bigger than on his picture," hissed Mason. "He's killed loads of people too," he added, more quietly.

"That looks like some kind of futuristic rifle," Lot added with a tremor of concern. "I guess that's the tech we're supposed to retrieve?"

Dev realized they were waiting on his instructions. He cursed the fact that his uncle had forbidden him from taking the Iron Fist mech suit, something that was designed to go up against weapons that would otherwise easily kill them. The kitbag Eema had provided was a joke when it came to weapons.

Christen finished assembling the gun, thumbed a button, and easily lifted it up, aiming it at the tower. The rifle whined to life, and the orb hanging from the barrel began to glow. From the indicators on the barrel, it was clearly charging up.

"Dev. . .?" urged Lot.

Dev gathered his courage. He pulled the plastic cylinder of what looked like marbles from the kitbag and stepped forward.

"Hey, you!" In retrospect, Dev realized it wasn't the most intimidating opener he could have come up with.

Christen turned his head and frowned. "Beat it, kid."

"I can't let you do . . . whatever it is you're doing," said Dev lamely. He sounded like the worst cop in the world.

Christen laughed and turned his attention back to

the building. The rifle had nearly finished powering to life, forcing the big man to shoulder the weapon's rapidly increasing weight.

Frustrated, Dev looked to his friends for support. Mason gave a toothy smile, a thumbs up and a nod of encouragement.

Dev took out the *SHOK-BALLS!*[TM] container, gave it a short, sharp shake, then spilled the contents towards Christen. A dozen steel balls rolled along the pavement. The moment they hit Christen's feet a powerful spark zapped out and struck his ankle.

Christen howled in pain, stepped back on to another ball – and received another powerful shock. He stumbled, triggering more and more of the *SHOK-BALLS!*[TM] in a succession of jagged orange sparks. The sparks from the balls were so powerful that the bottom of Christen's trousers began to smoke and smoulder. Dev could see why the balls were banned.

Still, Christen kept his balance and didn't drop the gun. Instead he turned the barrel towards Dev, his mocking smile now replaced with an expression of rage.

He pulled the trigger.

Dev hit the deck a fraction of a second before a shimmering wave of gravitons passed overhead. It arced across the plaza and struck the bus. Dev waited for an explosion, but instead he watched in surprise as the bus lifted into the air, still encased in the shimmering beam. The panicking driver just had time to leap from the open door as Christen moved the gun – effortlessly guiding the bus through the air.

Straight towards Dev.

Christen controlled the range using a small toggle next to the trigger, drawing the vehicle closer – and then swung the entire gun down, mimicking the strike of a hammer.

Dev threw himself against a low wall as the bus crashed down with such force that the front quarter of it concertinaed into a mass of twisted metal and smashed glass. He felt the rush of air from the impact, and threw his arms over his head to protect himself from the shower of safety glass. Luckily the wall took the force of the impact; otherwise, Dev would have become a pancake.

With a bellow, Christen angled the gun, raising the bus high in the air. Clearly he wasn't finished with it – or Dev.

"Hey, idiot!" screamed Lot, waving her arms over her head. "Over here!"

Christen scythed the gun in an arc sideways, and the crumpled vehicle flew through the air in a corresponding motion, centimetres off the ground.

Lot and Mason ran for their lives as the bus, now angled on its side, smashed several lamp posts, trees and a couple of benches as it thundered straight towards them. They reached the safety of the train station entrance just as the bus crumpled sidelong into the building – too large to fit through the gap.

Christen used the thumb-toggle to try and change his angle of attack. He was so engrossed that he didn't notice Dev had run up behind him. Dev flung himself at Christen, and he managed to lay a hand on the gun. In the split second of contact, Dev invoked his synaesthesia, communicating directly to the electronic systems of the weapon. Information flooded into his mind – the name Newton's Arrow, the weapon's serial number, what each component did to manipulate gravitons that formed the shimmering beam—

There was a bright flash in Dev's mind's eye. Ordinarily he received the technical feedback as a pleasant mix of colours and sound, but this flash was painful, like having an instant migraine. He slammed into Christen's back, but barely moved the straining, massive man from his standing position. Dev fell to the ground and, still reeling from the jolt, scurried backwards in confusion.

At that moment he noticed two things at the same time. There was a second man standing across the street, half hidden by the shadows. His stance was so relaxed – just a casual observer to the chaos unfolding – that Dev wondered whether he'd been there the whole time. The second thing was that Christen had turned around and reoriented the barrel towards Dev.

Dev ran for his life. The Mode Gakuen Cocoon Tower was the closest thing that could feasibly provide cover. After a few long strides, he felt his leg muscles burn as he jumped . . . and he was propelled a full storey up, where his fingers managed to grab hold of a narrow metal ledge that formed the external structure. It was an impossible jump for his friends, but not for Dev. At birth he had been given more abilities than just his special synaesthesia, including a boost in strength and speed in moments of crisis. It was almost a superpower – if superpowers only lasted for one go before requiring rest to recover their strength again.

But it was enough to take Christen by surprise. Christen jerked back, pulling the trigger. The graviton beam missed Dev, striking the base of the building instead. There was a horrendous screech of tortured metal and a crunch of concrete as the entire fifty-storey building was ripped off its foundations. It rose five metres in the air, with Dev still clinging to a piece of steel lattice.

In panic, Dev let go. He crashed into one of the still-standing trees in the plaza, the branches snapping under his weight, and he bounced painfully to the ground. His head spun, as did the building above him. His vision blurred, but he caught sight of Christen straining as he moved the entire building with just his control of the gun.

Dev looked down at his crumpled body, and he tried to move, but everything ached after his super-jump. Nothing seemed broken, at least. Then he heard the sound of the van engine squealing away, and he managed to sit up as Mason and Lot caught up with him.

"Dev? Dev? Can you speak?"

The sound of police sirens cut through the air, and Dev slowly, painfully stood up, broken twigs flaking off his sore body. "Where is he?"

Not only had Christen gone, but so too had the entire Cocoon Tower.

Dev dreaded trying to explain *that* to his uncle.

WHAT GOES UP...

"He stole an entire building!" said Dev with despair.

"Well, how hard can it be to find him, then?" asked Mason, scratching his head thoughtfully. "I mean, it's a flying building! And if I learned anything in physics, it's what goes up has got to come down."

The three teens had fled the scene moments before the police cars had arrived. They were pretty sure none of their explanations would have been believed, and they had most definitely failed to follow Charles Parker's order to not draw attention to the stolen technology. Lot and Mason had tried to get to Dev, and by the time the van had pulled away, their view of the floating Cocoon

Tower had been blocked by the high-rise buildings around them.

They were headed back towards the park, debating whether they should stay in Japan to track down Christen or return home ... and face being told off by Charles. They decided to stay and attempt to fix the problem.

But that didn't stop Charles from contacting them. "How could you—?" he began, his face glaring from the screen on Dev's phone.

But Dev was quick to cut him off. "Where were you? How could you send us out against a madman, only armed with a bag of shocking marbles, when he had some sort of gravity gun?"

Charles Parker wasn't used to being shouted at, so he tripped over his words. "W-we had n-no idea what he was, um, using."

"Newton's Arrow. Does that ring any bells?"

Charles Parker was silent for a long moment. He barely moved, and Dev began to wonder if the image was frozen, buffering. Then Charles's eyes twitched, and it became clear he was reading from another screen.

Charles's voice dropped with deep concern. "Dev, I'm sorry, I had no idea..."

Dev tried to hide his shock: his uncle rarely apologized. He briefly considered mentioning the weird sensation he'd experienced while trying to deactivate the device. The more he thought about it, the more he felt as if he had been deliberately blocked. Was it somehow connected to the man in the shadows, or had he simply been an innocent passer-by? He decided not to mention it; he didn't want to cause a fuss, when there might be no reason for one.

"So, Newton's Arrow," said Lot in her matter-of-fact way, "it plays around with gravity?"

"Specifically gravitons," Charles corrected. "It's not just about whether or not you stick to the ground; it's much more complicated. Newton's Arrow is a very dangerous prototype weapon that had been locked away in the Red Zone."

"And he used it to steal a building," said Mason, shaking his head. "I mean, who does that?"

"You have a point," agreed Charles.

"I do?"

"Certainly. Why steal an entire building if you only wanted something inside? Then again, why steal a building in a quieter part of the city if you're doing it to make a statement?"

"He's a criminal," said Dev. "That's what they do. I thought our job was to retrieve the tech, not get involved in solving weird crimes."

Charles Parker sighed and nodded. "You are correct. You're a repo team; that's your mission. The priority now is to find the Arrow and return it before this madman can create any more mayhem."

"And how do we find him?"

"Easy. Look for the fifty-storey tower block he's walking around with."

Charles Parker deactivated the video link and turned to Sergeant Wade.

"You still think they don't require my help?" she asked.

Charles shook his head. "So far, so good."

Wade frowned. "And what happens when things begin to escalate beyond our control?"

Charles's attention was on a screen filled with scrolling information, his response sounding almost too casual: "They won't. We'll make sure things don't slip from our grasp. We have laid the bait, now let's just wait for the trap to spring." He quickly typed something on the keyboard, then hit a button to shut down the screen just as Wade leaned over to read it. Charles stood. "If you'll excuse me, I am needed elsewhere."

Without another word he marched from the room, followed moments later by Eema rolling close on his heels like a giant metallic boulder – or constant bodyguard.

"Is it my imagination, or is your uncle completely useless?" asked Mason the moment Charles Parker disconnected.

Dev sighed. "Welcome to my world."

Lot found local news stations on her Inventory phone. Sure enough, sightings of a floating building over Tokyo were already trending across the news.

Their translator earpieces allowed them to understand the basics of the reports, although Dev was a little dismayed when his translator seemed to possess a life of its own.

"Be gone the mighty fish!" declared one reporter, who was filming the area from a helicopter.

Dev tapped his fingers against his ear. "I think the battery is running low."

"Found it!" Lot stopped on another news channel that showed the stolen building. She attempted to turn her screen because it looked like the tower was lying on its side – before she realized it really was lying horizontally on the ground. A helpful map showed just how far Christen had got.

"That's not too far from here," Mason pointed out.

"Lowering electric monkey results in crash!" declared the excited news reporter in Dev's ear, but oddly he got the gist.

"I bet Christen ran out of battery!" said Dev. "He had to drop it wherever he could!"

Mason laughed. "What an idiot. He didn't get that far after all."

"But I bet Christen is probably long gone in that case," said Lot. "And he still has the weapon."

The words were barely out of her mouth when the news camera zoomed in on movement within the building. Somebody was still inside, and the three friends had little doubt as to who it was.

Mason frowned. "Why didn't he just run away?"

"Because whatever's in the building is so important that he tried to steal the whole thing," said Dev. "He's not going to leave empty-handed. Which means we still have time to complete our mission."

TOPSY-TURVY

The surrounding area was awash with flashing lights from the emergency services that had cordoned the toppled building off from a massive crowd of spectators. Christen had dropped the building in the huge moat surrounding the Imperial Palace, a large park in the heart of the city that also included the royal family's home. The deep walls of the V-shaped moat had acted like a cradle to hold the building in place, although the structure was never designed to lie horizontally, so it had already started to crush the sides of the building touching the ground.

Luckily the royal family were out of the country, but

security had remained high. Police and news helicopters swarmed overhead, searchlights combing over the structure, looking for further signs of movement.

Dev, Lot and Mason watched from a distance, unable to push through the thick crowd of spectators. It was as close as they could get.

"Wouldn't it be easier to let the police capture him, and then they can hand over Newton's Arrow to us?" said Mason.

"For once I agree," said Lot. "There's no way we're getting through that lot unseen."

Dev shook his head. "We have a mission. It doesn't matter if this guy gets arrested or if we get whatever it is he's trying to get. We need to return the Newton's Arrow to the Inventory, and I can't see the Tokyo police handing over something like that to three foreign teens who don't even have passports." Dev almost bitterly added, *"And because that's my only purpose in life, the reason I was created."*

Mason tutted. "In case you didn't notice, there is no way we are getting close to the building without being spotted. It's impossible."

That made Dev smile. "Impossible is what we do best."

*

The beached Cocoon Tower was surrounded by amazed spectators, most of whom were recording the sight on their mobile phone cameras. It was being filmed from every direction, even from above, and broadcast live around the world. Approaching unseen would be inconceivable.

"This isn't going to work," growled Mason in a low voice.

Dev snapped back, "Shut up and keep walking."

The crowd before them parted like water, allowing the trio, all wearing dark sunglasses despite it being night-time, an unhindered path straight for the building. They were following a small blue light that floated ahead of them. It was the unremarkable AttentionGrabber from Mason's kitbag. Dev had taken a picture of it with his phone, and the Inventory database had identified it and provided instructions. Both hemispheres spun around in opposite directions, allowing it to slowly fly in whatever direction it was pushed. It emitted a flashing blue light that drew people's attention and scrambled their neurons, effectively instructing their brains to ignore the people closest to the light; it was a mild form of amnesia. Dev, Mason and Lot wore Inventory-issue shades from their kitbags, but even a cheap pair was protection enough for users to block the blue light's effects on their own brains. Luckily due to the late hour, nobody else in the crowd was wearing shades.

The teens were able to wirelessly command the Avro to hover high overhead, completely cloaked, while its stealth technology blanked every video recording below. Lot felt as if they were living ghosts, able to go anywhere.

Keeping up with the slow-moving AttentionGrabber, they walked straight up to the police cordon, ducking under the tape, and straight past the glazed expression of the policeman standing guard. They clambered through a broken window as Dev plucked the AttentionGrabber from the air and pocketed it.

Inside it was dark, completely without power; the electricity cables had been severed the moment Christen had raised the building into the air. The noises from the street were muffled, replaced with the groaning and creaking of stressed metal as the building struggled to stay intact around them. Plaster dust trickled down like fitful snow, and the occasional tremor sent cracks splitting across the walls.

"My head is spinning already," said Dev as they looked around. The Inventory shades they wore were no ordinary ones; the lenses in them amplified light, even if there was very little, transforming the darkest hole into a crisp world of grey.

Because the building was lying on its side, office furniture had slid across the carpeted floor and piled up against one wall – the new floor. The desks and chairs made a handy hill they could scramble up to reach the door, which was now in the ceiling.

The ascent up the desk-hill was punctuated by alarming moments when the furniture seemed to shift under their weight, threatening to topple. They cautiously made it the doorway, which was now more of a hatch, as if accessing a loft space. They reached up and hauled themselves into the corridor above.

Lot's voice echoed down the corridor. "Wow!"

Due to the topsy-turvy geography of the building, one branch of the T-junction corridor stretched upwards in a menacing shaft that had doorways on either side. It would be a horrendous climb if they needed to reach the centre of the building. The branching corridor in which they now sat on the floor, which was actually a corridor wall, ran along the bottom of the building. Every several metres there was a doorway in the "floor" – some were closed and could *probably* take their weight. Others were open, deadly pits that could swallow them whole. The same pattern was mirrored in the "ceiling", although these doorways were so near they could reach the handles with outstretched hands. The floor-wall itself was a shattered collection of plasterboard, which Mason had already put his leg through when he'd stepped on it. They had to be careful to keep to the studwork beneath that held their weight.

Eema's voice came over their headsets. "Dev, you asked what this building was used for. It housed a fashion design company——"

Mason grinned. "Boy, Christen must really be desperate for some new clothes."

"——and it was also the home of a technology company: NiGen Labs. It is located on the top floor."

Dev exchanged knowing looks with the other two. There was no chance of going back outside to try and re-enter the building further up, as the news feed on their phones showed them that the crowds had doubled outside; all it would take was the AttentionGrabber not working for a second and they would be caught. Plus, the top of the building curved upwards from the ground, meaning they would only gain a small advantage. No, the only way upwards, or rather sideways, was through the building itself.

Dev's further worry that they would have to climb up the imposing corridors was replaced when he mentally twisted the building in his mind's eye and realized the top floor was, at least partially, now on ground level. As they had approached the building along its length, he calculated they must be on the fifth floor already.

"That means we're going to have to smash our way through the ceiling," said Mason, who had also worked out the mind-bending geography.

Dev pointed to an elevator door in the "ceiling" a little further along the corridor. "Not if we can open that."

They gingerly leapt over an open doorway to reach the elevator door. Dev was the tallest, but his fingers still failed to gain purchase between the smooth metal doors.

"I need a piggyback to get higher."

"Don't look at me," said Lot.

With a sigh, Mason stooped down low. Dev climbed on to Mason's back, then wrapped his legs so tightly around Mason's shoulders and neck that he heard Mason gasp.

"I can't breathe!"

"Ssh!" Dev needed both hands. His fingertips were just small enough to prise open the doors. The doors grated as he did so, opening wide enough for him to hoist himself through.

Inside the sideways lift shaft, thick steel cables ran past Dev, back to the lift car that had been on the ground floor. His eyes, still enhanced by special lenses, followed the path of the cables – which now ran horizontally at chest height – to the giant winches at the end of the building. It looked a straightforward journey.

Lot was next. Dev offered his hand to help her through. Of course she was too determined to accept any help – other than placing her foot on Mason's head – to spring into the shaft. It took both of them to lift the heavier Mason in after themselves.

Dev beckoned for them to follow him further into the shaft. Their footsteps thudded against the solid elevator walls but echoed like barrel drums each time they crossed the hollow doors in the floor. Every few moments the building trembled, and there was a far-off creak of straining metal.

Soon they reached the uppermost floors. Dev put his finger over his lips, even though the others hadn't said anything. They stopped at a set of elevator doors in the floor, from which they could hear movement and muffled talking beyond. They exchanged worried looks, wondering if they were about to confront more than one bad guy.

"This is it," whispered Dev. He pulled the kitbag from his shoulder and unzipped it. "Let's keep this simple. We dart in, stun him, grab the gun and leave." He handed them several glass capsules. "Smoke bombs. Should create enough of a distraction, along with this." He took the AttentionGrabber from his pocket. "Ready?"

The others nodded. Mason gripped one edge of the door and Lot the other. On a silent count of three, they both heaved it open. Dev dropped the AttentionGrabber, the blue light flashing hypnotically into the room. He took a deep breath and dropped down.

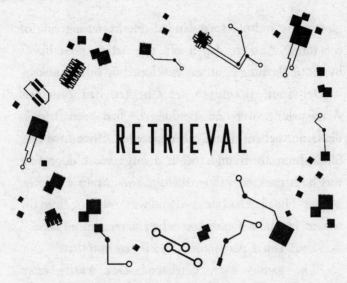

RETRIEVAL

The attack went wrong even before it really got started.

Dev dropped from the elevator door – which was now effectively in the ceiling of the room beyond. A mound of furniture, that had piled up on the floor when the building moved, broke his fall.

The instant Dev hit the furniture, Lot threw in a smoke bomb, which detonated with a bang. The sound took Dev completely by surprise; he had missed the explosive part of the smoke release when he had speed-read the item's description in the Inventory computer. The second mismanaged thing was that Lot had dropped the smoker without knowing where their bad guy was standing, so it landed on the wrong side of the room. And, to cap it off, the AttentionGrabber's hypnotic flashing light was enveloped by thick smoke.

Dev spun around to see Christen had Newton's Arrow slung over one shoulder; he had been hauling desks, leather sofas and other pieces of office furniture to position them underneath a large vault door that was built into the wall – which in this instance was the ceiling. The man had stopped and was coughing from the smoke. He did a double take when he recognized Dev.

"You? You're persistent, kid, I'll give you that."

"The game's over, Christen." Dev warily crept forward and pointed to the rifle. "That belongs to me."

Christen gave a pitying laugh and trained the gravity gun on the vault door in the ceiling above Dev. "And just how do you plan to get it off me?"

He fiddled with the rifle's selector controls and pulled the trigger. Nothing happened.

Christen irritably thumped the side of the weapon with his palm – and the power light blinked awake. He fired again.

A graviton pulse spat at the door. Christen had set the device for a specific task and, just as the battery died, it performed it admirably. The door began to creak as the gravity within it intensified, its atoms pulling on one another.

Dev took his chance to run for the gun once again. He needed physical contact with the device in order for his synaesthesia to work. But he had barely moved when there was an ear-splitting crack from the vault. The door only needed to contract by a centimetre for the lock and hinges to smash apart. The mini gravitational force was simply too powerful for mere steel. A second later the door buckled and fell down into the room with a heavy thud – and the contents of the vault cascaded out with it.

Dev rolled aside as the heavy door smashed down millimetres from his head. He was half buried in a wave of thick stacks of money as they rained down from the vault entrance, interspersed with notebooks, hard drives, paper files, boxes and other items.

Christen wasted no time in hunting through the safe's contents. He ignored the money and instead went straight for an unremarkable blue plastic box about the size of a large laptop. He snatched it up and shoved it into the knapsack he was wearing.

Mason and Lot dropped into the room with a battle cry, startling Christen, who had been focused on the task at hand.

"Drop everything!" bellowed Mason, holding up the BubbleBrella – the only thing in the kitbag that could possibly resemble a weapon. According to the Inventory database, it was really an energy shield designed to be used for protection in industrial environments by projecting a repulsive cone to prevent things from falling on to a worker's head. At first glance it looked just like any other telescopic umbrella Mason's mother would carry, which he had often pretended was a gun – at least when nobody else was around.

"What is this? A school trip?" snorted Christen. He turned his back on them and now started making his way towards a solid square metal box, about halfway up the mountain of money, the kind used to carry expensive electronic items.

Lot threw another smoke bomb – this one hit Christen square in the back. He yelped loudly as it exploded, enveloping him in a cloud of smoke.

"Great! Now we can't see him," hissed Mason.

Lot didn't care; it meant he couldn't see them, either. She rushed to find Dev. When the door had fallen, it looked as if it had crushed him, at least from her point of view in the ceiling's elevator shaft. She found him curled up on the floor.

"You're all right!" she said with relief.

Dev forced a smile and nodded, although he was shaken from the near miss.

"You brats just don't know when to quit, do you?" snarled Christen as he stepped from the smoke. In one hand he held the open flight case as the other extracted a slender battery pack. He discarded the case. "I was warned that someone would probably come and interfere, but they didn't tell me it would be kids." He slid the battery into an empty slot in Newton's Arrow. It came to life with a whine. "And I was instructed that if anyone were to turn up, to deal with them however I saw fit."

Dev, Lot and Mason were open targets. Mason waved the energy umbrella in what he hoped was a menacing way, but it did nothing to deter Christen.

"Now, I wouldn't normally bother with kids. But you three need to be taught a lesson."

He selected a setting on the gravity gun and aimed at the trio. He flashed a toothy grin, watching them tremble . . . then aimed the gun at the ceiling and fired.

The graviton pulse passed through the wall and to the other side of the building — moving through the walls, floors and ceilings. The moment it reached the exact distance Christen had programmed, the graviton stream imploded.

The effect was immediate. With a deafening noise, the entire building began to shake. Metal groaned and concrete dust poured down in waves. Then, as its centre of gravity shifted, the entire building began to *roll*.

Everything in the room began to tumble towards one wall – as it fast became the floor. Dev slipped as his current floor rolled to become a wall – and caught a brief glimpse of Christen laughing as he disappeared through a door.

Then a tsunami of furniture cascaded over the remaining trio as the room revolved around them.

At first the assembled crowd couldn't work out what was happening as the building began to roll. Their confusion soon gave way to utter panic as the oval-shaped tower impossibly rolled *out* of the moat that had been cradling it as its newly shifted centre of gravity toppled it over. The crowds gathered in the public gardens ran for their lives as the oval building lolloped like an enormous egg towards them. Cars and fire engines were effortlessly crushed, and trees splintered like twigs as the building ground through the thick ancient wall surrounding the Imperial Palace gardens. It crushed the last surviving samurai guardhouses in the gardens as well as the gift shop as the Cocoon rolled a full turn. Just as it seemed about to stop, it teetered ... before its newly displaced centre of gravity propelled it into yet another rolling cycle, like a rugby ball flipping end-over-end.

They would be crushed to death. Dev had little doubt about that.

The room swirled around them. A massive office desk slammed down over them, briefly sheltering them and taking the brunt of other furniture that would have flattened them. Their moment of safety was brief, as the room continued to roll and they were suddenly sliding towards the far wall, which had been their ceiling moments earlier.

And every item in the room coasted with them; furniture splintered and screeched as it moved. The building itself groaned and shrieked as it began to fall apart. It was a cacophony of destruction.

It was a miracle that Mason was still clutching the energy umbrella. Lot yelled to him, but the noise around them drowned her words. She reached over and plucked it from Mason's hand. Gripped the middle and twisted the lower section.

Dev's ears popped as a clear shield completely surrounded them in a sphere, projected from the pole in Lot's hand. She held it aloft, straining as items bounced heavily against the shield, but it didn't stop their bubble from ricocheting around the room in the building's tumble.

It was like being trapped in a hamster ball, stuck in a washing machine.

No heights had ever made Dev feel this ill.

Glass, chunks of concrete and shredded steel tore away from the Cocoon Tower as it rolled from the gardens – over the shallow moat on the opposite side of the palace – and across the street, leaving a deep rut in the earth and crushing traffic. The building sheared in two, unable to take the pressures exerted on it. Both halves rolled to an almost instant stop.

The moment the building fell silent, Dev and his friends pushed against the energy shield, knocking away debris pinning them down. Lights from the city outside could be seen through gigantic cracks in the wall.

Dev patted Lot on the back. "That was quick thinking."

Lot held up the device so that Mason could see the

logo etched on the side. "Learn to read!" she snapped at him.

"BubbleBrella?" he read. "How am I supposed to know what that does?"

"Guess!"

"And what if I guessed wrong?"

"Mase, when we're about to be killed, I think you can afford to take that chance."

Mason blushed; he didn't like being shouted at. He was the one with the fearsome image in school, but in reality he was a pushover when anybody stood up to him. Dev was even beginning to feel sorry for him … but assumed that was just a side effect from the motion sickness he was feeling.

Dev tapped his watch, sending instructions for the Avro to descend and pick them up.

They made their way through the office contents, most of which were now nothing more than unidentifiable pieces of broken wood and crushed metal. There was no way they should have survived that. They passed through a huge fissure in the wall and clambered down to the road below.

They had barely jumped on to the torn-up tarmac when the air next to them shimmered and a ramp extended seemingly from mid-air. They leapt aboard the Avro and flopped, exhausted, into their seats.

"Eema, take us home," said Dev with a heavy sigh. They had failed the mission, and part of downtown Tokyo was destroyed in the process. He would have to face his uncle's disappointment – again.

Lot folded her arms and sat back in her chair. "Why were we given the world's naffest gadgets to stop him with? If we had had the Iron Fist mech, none of this would have happened."

Her anger was directed at the disembodied Eema, and Dev found himself nodding in agreement. There was a pause before Eema replied.

"Charles Parker judged that the mech suit should remain in the Red Zone like all other retrieved items posing such danger. He deems the suit to be of great value."

The silence that descended on the room was so intense that Dev thought he could hear the blood pounding in his ears. He was angry enough for it to pump harder.

"But our lives are not?" he snapped back.

Eema's silence was all the confirmation he needed.

DOUBLE DEAL

Christen closed his eyes and breathed in the clear sea air as the yacht raced across Tokyo harbour. It blew away the dust clinging to his face. A flute of champagne was pushed into his hand.

"Congratulations."

Christen took the glass and studied Kardach, noticing that he wasn't drinking. Kardach was watching the receding city lights, and Christen took the opportunity to discreetly toss the sparkling liquid over the side, just in case his host was not happy about how things had turned out. Champagne with a few drops of poison: that was how the criminal underclass rolled.

"It was not my fault the weapon's stupid battery chose that moment to die."

Kardach shrugged. "Nobody said it was. No need to be so defensive." He smiled when he saw Christen scowl. "Perhaps you had one too many practice shots? Who knows?" Christen's eyes narrowed as Kardach tried to pass the blame. "However, you certainly made a statement back there. And that is all for the good."

"What was the statement, exactly?"

Kardach smiled. "Don't mess with us. I think that's was pretty clear. And you got what we needed."

"Spares for the gun, and this. . ." He held up the blue case. Kardach reached for it – and Christen instinctively pulled it from his grasp. Kardach reached again, and the killer look on Kardach's face ensured Christen didn't try pulling away a second time. "So what's so important about that?"

"That is not the concern of either you or me."

"Ah, your big bad boss man. . ."

"A boss man who is very happy with you for the moment." Kardach said it with a smile, but Christen was smart enough to understand the underlying threat: *for the moment.*

"And those kids. . .? I told ya I don't like harming kids. Usually," he added as an afterthought.

Kardach waved his hand dismissively. "Don't worry about them. They deserved what they got. Besides, they walked away unharmed." He ignored the curious look on the gangster's face and continued. "We have another proposition for you. One the *boss man* would like to explain face to face."

Christen's eyes widened. "I get to meet Double Helix himself?"

Kardach nodded. "You are invited to officially join Shadow Helix. The universe's greatest treasures await you. All you have to do is say yes."

Kardach extended his hand. Christen looked at it for a moment. Shadow Helix, one of the world's most notorious and secretive criminal organizations. No, one of *history's*, he corrected himself. All he had to do was shake hands and he would be welcomed into the fold. He had never before known anybody who had joined those ranks.

And that in itself should have raised alarm bells for him. . .

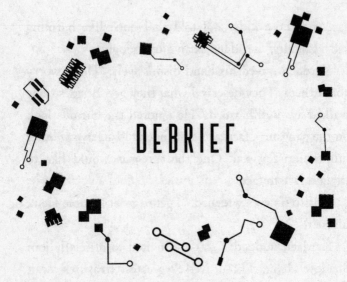

DEBRIEF

Dev slouched back in his chair and ran through the recent events in his mind.

Their lives had been risked for nothing. Christen was no normal thug, he was sure of that. He was surprised that such a powerful weapon had not been properly catalogued by his uncle, a man who noticed the slightest thing Dev put out of place in the miles of Inventory shelving. He was also bothered by the reaction he had experienced when he had touched the weapon. It was quite unlike anything he had experienced before. What had caused it?

Again his focus shifted to what Christen had been

searching for in the vault – the blue plastic case. What was in it? A thought danced on the edge of Dev's mind, one he couldn't quite grasp. . .

They were seated in the Inventory canteen as his uncle listened to Lot's telling of their tale. Mason had devoured a burger and was now slurping on a strawberry milkshake. Lot had requested green tea, which Dev thought was rather sophisticated. He had a cola, but he had yet to take a sip and it was already becoming a flat, syrupy mess.

"If we'd had the Iron Fist mech, it would have been easier—" Dev began.

Charles Parker sighed to cut him off and gently drummed his fingers on the table, a habit that signalled that he was stressed. "Eema selected a range of easy-to-carry devices that could help if used . . . *creatively*."

"But—"

"The mech is too powerful an artefact, Dev. You already proved that in Canada. If it fell into the wrong hands. . ." He shook his head. "It's safer here. Plus, if you had damaged it. . ."

"What if *we* had been damaged?" Mason piped up. He looked away when Charles fixed him with an icy stare.

Growing up in the Inventory, Dev had learned to

parse his uncle's use of unofficial terms referring to the items. *Artefacts* were his most precious exhibits, *devices* had specific uses, and *gadgets* tended to be smaller, could serve multiple functions and were, in his uncle's opinion, less impressive. Items branded *gizmos* tended to be things his uncle didn't see the point of, such as fun toys.

"Well, it's a good job we're creative," said Lot quietly. "Otherwise we'd have been squished."

Charles smiled and nodded, completely missing the bitterness in her voice. "Exactly. It shows that you are the right people for this job after all. Trust me, there are many soldiers under Sergeant Wade's command who would have crumbled under the pressure. You didn't."

Lot looked away. She enjoyed the compliment, but refused to show it.

Dev leaned forward, determined not to be swayed by his uncle's unexpected compliments. "Now you know what we're up against. Newton's Arrow. Just give me the Iron Fist mech, and we can get it back."

"Yeah," said Mason, finishing the last of his milkshake with a loud slurp. "It's not as though we can cause more damage than what just happened. And if you happen to have a second suit . . . I wouldn't mind. . ." he added hopefully, but trailed off when he saw Charles Parker's face pinch.

"The suit has no protection against a gravity weapon."

"Neither do we," said Dev pointedly. He didn't know why, but he wanted to hear his uncle admit that he cared more about his precious Inventory items than he did them.

Charles pushed a tablet computer to the middle of the table. A holographic image of the Newton's Arrow rifle floated over the screen.

"First designed in 1968, by a friend of the World Consortium: Professor Haun Liu. An amazing engineer, he founded NiGen Labs in Hong Kong. He understood technology like no one else." Charles shook his head, his voice lowering with a level of respect that Dev had never heard from him before.

"Hero-worship alarm," muttered Mason, and Lot giggled.

Charles ignored them, continuing, "Newton's Arrow harnesses gravitons, a fundamental weak force that mainstream science has yet to accept."

Lot frowned. "Weak force? I thought gravity kept us stuck to the planet and made the solar system orbit the sun. That's hardly weak."

"And what about black holes?" added Mason. "They destroy everything."

Charles Parker stood. "Let me demonstrate how easy it is to break the entire planet's gravity field. Are you ready?"

They nodded, expecting him to launch into an explanation about some complex gadget.

Instead he hopped on one foot. "There you go. A simple hop, and I can resist the entire pull of the earth."

Dev frowned as his uncle sat back down. "But we've had tons of gravity devices go through these doors. Take the Avro; isn't it powered by negative-gravity engines?"

Mason passed his hand over his head, accompanied by a swooshing sound, to indicate his incomprehension.

Charles noted Mason's bewildered expression. "It doesn't matter. Just accept that gravity is unlike any other force in the universe. Drop the tiniest measure of poison in a lake and you won't be harmed if you swallow some of the water. Take a concentrated dose and drop it in your milkshake" – Mason paused; he still had the straw in his mouth – "and there will be no hope for you."

Charles waved a hand towards the revolving Newton's Arrow graphic. "This device harnesses gravitons and unleashes them in concentrated, controllable waves.

Able to pass through anything — including entire planets — the waves created by this weapon can create localized gravity fields."

"Which is how he shrank the vault door," said Dev.

"Exactly. Or lifted an entire building, by creating an inverse-gravity field. This is a fascinating area of science that Professor Liu pioneered."

Dev had a thought: "Is Liu dead?"

"Retired. Once he realized just how destructive his research was, he disappeared into obscurity."

Lot tapped the holographic Newton's Arrow and watched it spin around. "So what we have here sounds like the ultimate weapon."

Charles nodded.

"Then why bother attacking a building?"

Charles Parker leaned back in his chair and steepled his fingers. "Now we come to the real issue."

One of the clues Dev had overlooked suddenly dropped into place. "You said NiGen Labs was Professor Liu's company?" he said, pointing at the holograph. "That explains why there was a spare battery in the vault. It's not as if this thing runs on a bunch of double As."

"Very astute, Devon. You are correct, although it is

not a battery in the traditional sense. It is a graviton amplifier, but effectively the same thing."

Dev continued. "So he hoped to take the building somewhere safe because he wanted the *entire* lab – he needed time to go through all the research in there." Charles nodded. "But the Arrow ran out of power."

Lot gasped, because she had just had a realization – at the same time as Dev.

Mason, however, looked between them, puzzled.

"They built the weapon, yeah?" Lot said to him. "They would have had all the plans, yeah?" She saw the penny drop.

"They could've made more of them!"

Charles nodded. "But thanks to you, he didn't get everything. We now have the blueprints safely stored away. You stopped him getting away with a lot of precious information."

"Except whatever was in that blue case," said Mason.

The faint ripples of satisfaction Dev had been feeling were suddenly extinguished. His uncle's expression became grim once more.

"Yes."

Dev studied his uncle's face. "What's in the case?"

"We don't know. It's a mystery to me." The moment

the words were out of Charles's mouth, Dev knew they were a lie. Or at least a partial lie. Charles's hand reached out and shut down the tablet's holographic display, and he looked over at Lot and Mason. "I believe it's time to get you both home. You must be exhausted."

Lot and Mason murmured in agreement. They shuffled out of the canteen, and Dev stood to leave.

"Devon, while you were out there ... did you see anybody else?" Charles asked. "Anybody who may have been assisting Christen Sandberg?"

Dev unwaveringly met his uncle's gaze. "Only who I told you. We think he drove the van on his own, so he had no accomplices." Dev had deliberately not mentioned the shadowy figure he had seen watching him, or the painful incident that had interfered with his synaesthesia.

Charles nodded. "Then I suppose we let the mystery continue."

No, thought Dev, *let's not...*

ENTER
THE HELIX

A rumbling sound grew, echoing along the metal walls, as they made their way down the corridor. Christen tried to project an air of confidence, but he was feeling more anxious than ever before.

Kardach led him off the yacht to a waiting helicopter. From there they travelled in complete darkness for over an hour. When they landed, Christen couldn't see a thing, but the lingering smell of salt air convinced him they were still close to the ocean.

They entered a huge room with oak-panelled walls, each of which was decorated with a distinctive twirling logo. Christen had first thought it illustrated a pair of spiral staircases, but then he remembered where he had seen it before: it was a double helix, representing the strands of DNA that made all life possible. His new, mysterious master had adopted both the name and image.

A lone figure sat at the end of a table so long that fifty people could sit either side. Christen had no doubt the man at the end was Double Helix. He was expecting an archetypal villain, somebody who belonged more in a movie than in real life. Instead, Double Helix looked ordinary, plain, like the kind of person Christen would expect to run a church jumble sale.

Helix slowly stirred a cup of tea; the spoon gently tinkled each time it touched the fine china porcelain. Then he spoke in an unassuming voice. "Mr Sandberg. Welcome to Shadow Helix." He nodded towards Kardach. "My associate here told me how marvellously well you performed in Japan."

Christen grinned. "It was a blast. And you paid very well, sir." He had no idea where *sir* came from. He'd never called anybody sir, except when he had been in school. Somehow it seemed the correct thing to do here.

"Indeed. Although there comes a time in a person's life when he must choose between money and something far greater."

Christen was baffled as to what could be more important than money.

Helix sensed his uncertainty and chuckled. "Believe me, there are many more things worth fighting for."

"I would like to know what they are," said Christen with complete honesty.

"Good. That is why I would be pleased if you joined my organization. After a recent . . . *incident*, I find myself a little short on key personnel."

"That's why I'm here."

Helix tapped his spoon twice on the edge of his cup as he finished stirring. "You may find some of the tasks unpalatable, but they must be completed without question."

"Of course."

"Good." Double Helix sipped his tea, then waved his cup towards Kardach. "My associate has all the information you require."

Kardach handed him a small phone. "All the details are on this. It's a retrieval job. It may involve a spot of assassination. I hope you don't mind."

Christen gave a broad, toothy grin. That had never stopped him before.

EAVESDROPPING

Dev tiptoed down the empty, curving corridor, one of many interlocking passageways that connected areas of the Inventory together in a series of increasingly secure rings. There had always been security cameras and monitors everywhere, but since the Collector's team had broken in, the World Consortium had vastly increased the surveillance, determined that that would never happen again. Or at least, that had been their plan.

Dev knew the security team were running behind schedule and, because the most important artefacts in the collection had already been stolen, there was little effort made for installing state-of-the-art security on half-empty shelves. Instead they had concentrated on preventing access from the outside.

Previously, Dev had created a clever computer code to trick the security system into not reporting his whereabouts, but that wouldn't work now, as Eema had been reprogrammed to respond to any hack on her system. Instead he used his special power to attack the hardware, convincing the camera processor to replace his image with the image of Charles Parker instead. Why rewrite the software code when his synaesthesia could help him rework the entire microprocessor hardware?

Dev opened the door to the Green Zone and made his way through the rows of shelves. It had taken minutes for the thieves to loot the most precious items, and his uncle and Sergeant Wade were still uncertain how they had managed to sort through and move so much so quickly.

Reaching a rack of remaining gadgets, Dev selected an OmniBoard so he could race through the zones quickly, balancing on the board's single orb-like wheel.

He made swift progress through the aisles of shelves, which seemed to get emptier the closer he got to the next inner sanctum: the Blue Zone.

The automated system, believing him to be Charles Parker riding an OmniBoard, opened the zone's giant access door. The last time Dev had been here, the entire hangar had been flooded with water as a security measure. Thankfully it was now bone dry. There were more items left here — enormous battleships and submarines held in dry-dock cradles, towering above him. He noticed some of the smaller craft had been taken, and there were several empty cradles, indicating entire battleships had been pilfered. Just how the thieves had managed that, he couldn't imagine.

Up ahead the door to the junkyard separated the warehouse units from the most secure area of all, the Red Zone, which lay at the heart of the Inventory. Dev's curiosity to know more about how he was created had turned into a nagging urge. He had questions he wanted answered, but his uncle had no intention of discussing the matter. He would have to find the answers himself — and that meant a second visit to the Red Zone.

Dev was dismayed to see several uniformed soldiers stationed outside the doors. His uncle clearly wasn't taking any chances, or perhaps he suspected Dev might try to enter. Whatever the reason, Dev was certain that if he caused anything to happen to the Consortium troops, he would be in major trouble. His mind raced, trying to figure out a way into the zone.

Suddenly, the door between sections hissed open and an electric Jeep drove through from the Red Zone side. Sergeant Wade was at the wheel, Dev's uncle sitting alongside. They briefly stopped to talk to the guards.

Dev ducked behind a tall pile of wooden packing crates, waiting until he heard the faint buzz of the approaching Jeep's electric engine. No sooner had the thought arisen in his mind that he wanted to know what his uncle and Wade were discussing than the Jeep shot past.

Dev instinctively pushed forward on the OmniBoard. He crouched low and reached out for the Jeep's rear bumper. He snagged it – and felt his arms almost yanked from their sockets as he was pulled along. He ducked low enough that he wouldn't be seen in Wade's mirrors. Thanks to the low buzz of the engine, he could hear their conversation perfectly.

"I have repeatedly told you how unhappy I am about using him. He shouldn't even be involved," said Wade in an angrier tone than Dev was used to hearing. She was usually so formal.

"I don't see what choice we have," his uncle replied.

"Shadow Helix is armed and dangerous. It's just a matter of time before they cause a major incident."

Dev was surprised. If Tokyo wasn't classed as a *major* incident, what was?

"I agree," said Wade. "But using *him* . . . that's the real danger. Can we really trust him?"

Dev frowned. Why wouldn't they trust him? Dev was completely trustworthy . . . even though he had bypassed security to snoop in an area he wasn't allowed to be in so he could spy on his uncle.

Mostly trustworthy, he corrected himself.

Charles Parker's answer caught Dev by surprise. "Of course I don't trust him. Wade, you make far too many assumptions. Stop treating him like a *real* person like you or me. He was made. A prototype. Nothing more than a biological gizmo like this lot."

Dev's arms suddenly felt weak, and he let go of the Jeep as it turned to leave the Blue Zone. He rolled to a quick stop behind a six-storey row of shelves.

His uncle had always been cool towards him, but those words cut like a knife to the heart. Dev could feel the tears rolling down his cheek. He'd heard it – a biological gizmo. The lowest of the low.

He wiped the tears away and looked back the way

they had come. The Red Zone held answers for him. And if they didn't trust him, fine. Then he had no reason to feel guilty about not following their rules.

He took a deep breath and wiped the last tear away. He was about to skate off when he suddenly heard his name. Nothing more than a whisper ... or was it his imagination?

No, there it was again. A muffled yet familiar whisper.

"Dev..."

He stepped closer to the shelves as his name was called again, a little louder.

"Where are you?"

"I am everywhere," came the voice. Dev placed his hand on a crate it seemed to be coming from, and felt it gently vibrate. As in the classroom, the voice was being projected into the warehouse in a way he couldn't understand. "You still seek answers, Dev."

"Yes."

"Your uncle is not the only person with answers."

"I suppose you are?"

The voice gently laughed.

"Of course, Dev. But there is somebody else you know who could help."

Dev frowned. "Who?"

No answer came. Dev traced his hand along the crate; the wooden surface was no longer vibrating. The mysterious voice had vanished, but Dev suddenly knew who would have the answers he sought.

Although he didn't like it.

THE NEED TO KNOW

Lot thought the noise was part of her dream . . . until she heard it again. Her eyes flicked open. The room was dark, but there was unmistakable movement in the shadows.

Someone was in her room.

She remained calm and waited for the intruder to make the first move. The figure leaned over her – and Lot allowed her instinct to kick in. She sprang from the bed, grabbing and twisting the figure's arm. Quickly shifting her weight, she threw him over her shoulder. The intruder cried out in pain and smashed into her wardrobe.

"Lot! Stop! It's me!"

She froze, recognizing the voice. She fumbled for the

light switch and burst out laughing when she saw Dev, groaning, in the split halves of her wardrobe doors, a torn poster of Australia falling over his head.

"What are you doing here?" she asked, pulling him up. "And look what you've done to my wardrobe! My dad'll go nuts!"

"I was trying to keep a low profile."

"Then why didn't you phone?"

"I don't know how extensively we're being watched. Phone calls can be recorded, traced – they can even pinpoint our exact location. I don't want to leave a trail."

"Watched? By whom?"

"My uncle, for one."

Lot frowned. "Wait, what's going on?"

Dev sat on the edge of the bed and gathered his thoughts. "My uncle is sending us out there to gather what was stolen. But he's not preparing us properly, is he? It's almost as if he doesn't want us to succeed."

"That's ridiculous," said Lot, sitting beside him.

"Is it? He's not telling us everything. He knows who is behind the Newton's Arrow attack and what's inside that blue case. So why doesn't he just say so? What are they hiding?"

Lot still didn't understand. Dev changed his approach.

"Unlike you, I was created."

"To guard the Inventory."

"Yes, but I think there is more to it than that, and I need your help to find out what."

Lot felt a wave of sympathy. She could see how lost Dev looked. "Why don't you simply sit down and ask your uncle?"

Dev pulled a face. "He really doesn't care. Trust me on that. I heard him talking to Wade. They don't trust me. To him, I'm just another gizmo." He almost didn't get the words out. He calmed himself. "They don't trust me, and I need answers."

He held up his phone. A 3D map floated above the screen, focusing on a small speck in the ocean. "Tartarus Prison. It belongs to the World Consortium, and they have somebody there I need to talk to."

Lot was horrified when she realized who he meant. "Ask Wade. Surely she would—"

"I don't trust her! This has to be done in secret. Please, I need your help."

Lot nodded. "OK. Have you told Mase yet?"

Dev smiled. "Not yet. But I'm looking forward to sneaking in and scaring the poop out of him!"

*

It was the easiest thing in the world for Dev, Lot and Mason to walk back into the Inventory, even after midnight. Their security badges allowed them to enter the underground bunker, and because the cameras still confused Dev with Charles Parker, no alarm was raised over the fact that the three were entering restricted areas unescorted.

Tricking the security into thinking Charles Parker was around also meant that they could pull items of equipment off the shelves, safe in the knowledge that no suspicions would be triggered by anybody watching a security monitor.

Every so often Mason would apologize to Dev. "Mate, I'm really sorry."

Dev touched his black eye and refused to look at Mason. "It's all right," he said, stuffing items into the kitbag.

"You really took me by surprise."

"It's my fault for sneaking in. I should have phoned you."

Dev also tried to avoid Lot's eye when she looked up from her phone.

"Well, yeah," Mason agreed. "That would've been better."

Dev zipped up the kitbag. "Now all we have to do is steal a ride."

This was the one aspect of the improvised plan that made Dev uncomfortable. The hangar was guarded at all times, and he had no desire to injure the poor Inventory crew stationed there. He just hoped they could be distracted for long enough.

Nobody stopped them from entering the hangar; in fact, a couple of technicians nodded in greeting, even though Dev had never been introduced to them. Luckily, due to the late hour, there were only a few people scattered around the enormous space.

The Avro sat in its dedicated space alongside the Eiodolon and several traditional helicopters used to ferry staff around. Unfortunately a uniformed guard stood in front of their aircraft.

"I wish we still had the AttentionGrabber," said Dev. That useful device was likely still being re-catalogued since their return from Tokyo, somewhere in the Inventory.

"So what are we going to do?" Lot whispered.

"Sing him a lullaby," replied Dev as he pulled what looked like a small megaphone from the kitbag. Originally marketed as a gadget to lull restless babies to sleep, it was soon banned when it was used during a jewellery heist.

Dev took aim and squeezed the trigger. Luckily he couldn't hear the concentrated sound wave due to the device's advanced acoustical design, but the guard could. It took several seconds before the guard gave a huge yawn, wobbled, then slumped down, fast asleep.

Dev, Lot and Mason didn't waste any time in running aboard the Avro. They took their seats, and the fluid control panel came to life in response. Lot gripped the flight controls.

"Are you sure you can fly this thing?" Mason asked for the dozenth time.

"Totally," said Lot, biting her lip. "We just need the hangar doors open."

Dev glanced at his watch. "Not a problem. . ."

With a slow, grinding noise, the hangar doors began to slowly open. Lot looked at Dev in surprise.

"How did you do that?"

Dev was about to boast, but instead decided to stick to the truth. He pointed upwards. "I checked the supply schedule."

Sure enough, a large Chinook helicopter began to descend through the rooftop doors.

"We have incoming!" yelled Mason.

They all looked at the screen just as Eema rolled into the hangar. The unconscious guard at the foot of the tail ramp gave them away immediately, and Dev cursed that they didn't take the time to hide the slumbering man.

"Lot — go now!" he commanded as he thumbed a button on the control panel to snap the access ramp closed.

Lot yanked back on the stick and twisted the throttle, and the Avro soared straight up. The helicopter was taking up most of the available room to escape.

Mason threw his arms over his eyes. "We're gonna crash!"

Gritting her teeth, Lot stomped on the pedals — flipping the disc around — and they shot through the narrow gap like a coin through a slot. There was a loud bang as the Avro's underbelly grazed the door, but they shot straight up with whoops of delight, narrowly missing the Chinook's powerful twin rotors.

DROPPING IN

What is it about heights? thought Dev. Why did they always have to be involved, no matter how hard he tried to avoid them? At least this time it was his own decision to be here.

Despite his churning stomach, he remained quiet and allowed Mason to vocalize the terror he was feeling.

"There's got to be an easier way to do this!"

Lot firmly shoved Mason's helmet on his head, the tinted visor blocking his frightened expression. "Oh, relax. It'll be fun!"

They all wore black full-body suits that were covered in scales the size of thumbs. At first glance they looked more like fish people. The outfits were rounded off with gloves and boots that shrank to fit them perfectly.

The Avro's ramp opened, revealing nothing but blackness below. Dev had been expecting the roar of wind he had heard on the Eiodolon, but there was nothing more than a brisk breeze.

"You're certain we're on target?"

Lot peeked over the edge. Unlike the others, she had a love of heights and an appetite for extreme sports. "Yup. I can just make out some lights down there."

Dev rested his helmet on top of his head but stopped short of putting it on. He looked at Lot, desperate for a crumb of comfort.

"You've done this before?"

Lot nodded and smiled. "Sure, a bunch of times with my dad. Only, we used parachutes."

She pushed his helmet on before securing her own. Mason's fast breathing could be heard across their headsets, then Lot's soothing voice:

"Hold hands." They did so, and Lot edged them down the ramp.

Dev was surprised to find himself quite relaxed. He mused that the advantage of leaping out of a hovering flying saucer at forty thousand feet in utter darkness was that he couldn't actually see what was happening.

"On three!" commanded Lot. "One, two—"

Dev felt a sudden yank on his arm as Lot pulled him and Mason over the edge. Within seconds his stomach fluttered in what was now becoming a familiar falling sensation.

Their jumpsuits immediately took over. The scales were adaptive surfaces that suddenly angled position, forming dozens of tiny wings across their bodies that sent them into perfect head-first dives towards their preprogrammed landing zone. Called PhantomSuits, they had been specially developed by the Chinese air force to allow special forces to HALO jump. High Altitude Low Opening was a form of military parachuting that meant troops wouldn't be detected on the way down, before special parachutes opened incredibly close to the ground, slowing them to a stop before impact.

Except PhantomSuits weren't your typical HALO jumping gear. For one thing, they didn't have parachutes.

Dev had originally proposed they land the Avro on the roofs below and find a way in from there. But Lot had had her eye on the PhantomSuits for a while and had read all about them on the Inventory's computers. She persuaded the guys that there was a better way to reach their target. She assured them that they would get straight there with the minimum of fuss.

If leaping out of an aircraft without a parachute could be called *minimum*.

Dev was beginning to regret listening to her. Especially when a chime sounded in his helmet, indicating they had reached terminal velocity and were now free-falling at one hundred and twenty-two miles per hour. Not that he could hear it clearly with Mason screaming down one ear and Lot shrieking with delight down the other.

At first it seemed the island was barely getting closer – then just as suddenly it began rapidly growing in size. Another chime sounded, indicating when parachutes would normally be deployed on other HALO suits.

But still they fell.

Now Dev could see the structures of Tartarus Prison in the darkness below. A wall followed the perimeter of the small island, each side a vertical cliff on which fierce waves crashed. Within the walls, three circular buildings were connected by corridors, forming a triangle. To one side lay two helipads, the only way on or off the prison island. Dev saw everything in the kind of detail that only terror encouraged. He could even make out cracks on the concrete paving and patches of moss covering the buildings' roofs.

The micro-fins on their suits quickly morphed shape, steering them precisely for their target: the solid roof of one circular building.

Dev wanted to shut his eyes, but they remained wide open as he heard a chime indicating impact – a second before he hit the roof.

The PhantomSuit earned its name. The moment they hit the roof, they phased straight through. Dev could feel the cold concrete passing through him. It was a fleeting experience because they were travelling so fast, and they hit the floor of the first room less than half a second later. They phased through that and continued ploughing through solid earth. Dev could even taste the soil in his mouth, feel the grains of dirt passing between his own body's cells. It was uncomfortable to say the least.

The dirt suddenly gave way to the concrete of the subterranean tunnels. Each successive floor felt as if they were splashing into water – and each transition slowed them rapidly down, so by the time they had reached their destination, they gently drifted through the ceiling and, with a final chime sounding to signal arrival at their destination, they dropped to the solid concrete as if they'd jumped off stools.

Lot was the first to take off her helmet, and she had to force herself not to cackle with delight. Dev was relieved to remove his; he was sweating heavily. Mason dropped his helmet to the ground and hunched over in the corner, where he was violently sick.

"Now these things definitely belong *inside* the Inventory," said Dev, catching his breath. He took in their new surroundings. They were in a semicircular room, with the only access door behind them. The room was split in half by a large plastic screen, behind which stood—

"Hello, Dev," said the Collector with a vague hint of a smile. "And you have brought your friends too. How nice."

Lot's smile evaporated now that she was face to face with the fiend who had orchestrated the attack on the Inventory. Although she had had minimal contact with him, she still retained a healthy fear.

Dev wasn't so afraid; after all, he had beaten the

Collector before. "You're not too surprised to see us dropping in like this?"

"I would have been surprised if you had brought a cake." He gestured to several security cameras that covered every angle of the room. "I take it you have disabled the cameras?" Dev nodded. "And I admire your method of entry. PhantomSuits. Good choice."

"That was my idea," said Lot as she crossed over to Mason, who was still hunched over, and gently rubbed his back. They both kept a wary eye on the Collector.

"I suppose you are here because you have pressing questions that Charles refuses to answer." Dev couldn't keep the surprise off his face. The Collector chuckled. "Don't forget, Dev, we are practically brothers. Good old Uncle Parker created you to replace me." He gestured to himself. "A tired old prototype."

Dev couldn't resist a sounding smug. "I am a *better* version of you."

The Collector nodded. If he was offended, he didn't show it. "I am not your enemy, Dev. After all, I am the closest thing you have to family."

"If that is the case, then answer my questions."

The Collector moved his hand, inviting Dev to take a seat at the table.

133

"You worked for Shadow Helix when you raided the Inventory. Where did the stolen items go?"

"All around the world. Shadow Helix is a global network."

"So they must have a base, a headquarters. Where is it?"

The Collector tapped his wrist where he would normally wear a watch. "You're asking the wrong questions, Dev, and time is sorely against you."

Lot and Mason exchanged a look and pulled out their phones to access the Inventory network.

Dev thought carefully. "Double Helix is running the show." A nod from the Collector. "So why is he handing the technology over to a bunch of criminals? Street thugs who robbed a bank. A South African crime lord who stole a building. Why not just hold the world to ransom and get on with it?"

The Collector laughed. "Because that's not how the world works, Dev. Helix is a strategist. Stop thinking of time in such a boring way. Events that are occurring now are merely echoes of what he planned long ago."

"Dev!" said Lot urgently. "Eema is trying something new to remotely access the Avro."

Dev had used his power to isolate the disc from any

form of remote control, so he was satisfied her efforts would be in vain.

"Ah, you took a craft out for a joyride?" said the Collector knowingly. "Daddy is going to be very angry."

Mason piped up. "They're trying to trace us."

Dev replayed the Collector's words in his head.

"So you are saying those events are linked?"

"Of course. Nothing he does is random. Those thieves in the bank. What did they steal?"

Dev shook his head, recalling the scene on top of the CN Tower as the money spilled from the thieves' bag.

"Cash."

"Hardly seems worth the effort, does it? To enable some thieves to rob a bank when another thug has a gravity gun that could have broken into Fort Knox."

"The bank robbery was a decoy."

The Collector clapped his hands. "Now you are thinking."

"Why would they want to draw attention to themselves?"

Lot had been listening to every word. She stepped next to Dev. "So we would come."

The Collector pointed a finger at Dev. "Yes, or more specifically, *you*."

"But they didn't get anything from me."

The Collector turned away from the glass and began walking in a slow circle. "Really? *Think*, Dev."

Lot looked around with a frown. "Did you feel that?"

Dev didn't feel anything. He was trying to remember the exact sequence of events. "Nothing happened. I caught them. One guy knocked me out for a second, but. . ."

"Knocked you out," the Collector repeated, with meaning.

Lot walked around the room – then stopped and looked sharply at Dev. "Surely you felt that?"

He had. As if the entire room had trembled.

"Ah, I fear time is running out. And you never even had time to ask me about the Black Zone. Or what our beloved uncle does to his pet projects that stray off their leashes."

Dev's mind reeled in confusion. "What?"

"You were not knocked unconscious. This power you have, this synaesthesia, it is not all one way."

Dev looked at his gloved hand. He tried to imagine exactly what the Collector meant. He hadn't noticed that the villain had moved to the very back of his cell.

"Tartarus is the most secure prison facility on the

planet. Highly secretive and, I assure you, a *complete* mystery for Shadow Helix. There was no hope that they would find me here. . ."

Now Dev understood. "Unless they were led here by somebody. I'm carrying a homing beacon. Those thieves gave me a virus!"

The Collector shrugged. Dev now understood – at the very moment the roof was sucked away with an ear-piercing crunch, as if a tornado had swept it up, and the Collector's rescue team dropped into the room.

TRAPPED!

The remains of the upper five storeys of the prison complex swirled in a maelstrom above their heads. A five-floor column of earth had been scooped out in seconds, next to which stood Christen, controlling the swarm of debris with Newton's Arrow.

With the ceiling removed, the transparent screen between Dev and the Collector just fell away. The rescue team had dropped in on streaming energy ropes, and before their boots had touched ground and the energy ropes had vanished, alarms had begun to sound across the complex.

One well-built man dropped in front of Dev and

stared at him. There was something very familiar about him.

"Ah, Kardach," said the Collector, stepping forward. "I believe you met Devon in Tokyo?"

It clicked in Dev's mind: the silent watcher in the shadows. And while Dev hesitated, Mason didn't have such reservations. His reactions were fast, and he pulled a weapon from his back – a net-gun, one of the few weapons remaining in the Inventory – and took aim.

Kardach didn't even look at him. He raised one hand as Mason pulled the trigger. The trigger moved, but the weapon was dead in Mason's hands. Lot raised a taser, but it too failed to fire.

Kardach then gestured towards the squawking sirens. As he clenched his fists the alarm fell silent.

The Collector regarded Dev critically. "Thank you for releasing me. You'll be pleased to know that I have no further use for you. I fear after this your uncle will decide that you're redundant. That is exactly what he thought of me. Dissolution awaits you, so this will be the last time we meet. After all, you were already replaced." He gestured towards Kardach. "Another project I released from the Inventory."

Streaming energy ropes, made from pure light,

shot down from above. The rescue team touched them and were instantly conveyed upwards, out of the pit. Kardach went next. The Collector touched his brow in a final salute before following.

No sooner had they cleared the pit than Christen deactivated the gravity field and the rubble thundered down.

Dev shoved Mason and Lot towards the heavy door frame as hundreds of tons of debris slammed into the room. The air was filled with dust and the remaining lights died, plunging them into darkness.

They were entombed alive.

The Collector took a deep breath of fresh air, the first he'd had since he was captured. The sound of energy weapons blasting in the darkness could be heard all around as his rescue team kept the prison guards at bay.

With his enhanced vision, darkness was no blindfold, and the Collector could see everything. A pair of rescue choppers, running with no lights, sat on the helipad, rotors still whirling. Anti-aircraft missile launchers hung limply on prison walls, deactivated the moment Kardach had closed in. They didn't stand a chance against Shadow Helix's superior forces.

The Collector headed straight for the helicopters, Kardach close by his side. "Did you have to bury the children?" the Collector asked, unable to disguise a hint of annoyance.

"We had our orders," Kardach replied, glancing at Christen, who followed a few steps behind.

They reached a chopper and boarded without another word. Within seconds they lifted into the darkness, and the rescue team followed in the second aircraft.

It took a few more moments before the prison guards emerged from safety and began shooting, far too late, at the receding aircraft.

Finally, thought Dev with a macabre hint of satisfaction, they had found something that Lot hated. Confined spaces.

Pushed against a solid metal door, the trio had barely any space to move. They were wedged between several large chunks of rubble, sealed into their tiny tomb by hundreds of tons of dirt. The only light came from the dim HUD displays in the helmets they still clung to.

Already Lot was fighting to control her panic, gulping deep lungfuls of air. With every breath she took, Mason's concern that she would use up all the oxygen increased.

"If I die because you suffocate us..." Mason stumbled for a suitably threatening conclusion. "I'll kill you," he finished lamely.

"Stop arguing," snapped Dev. "You're using up the air."

Lot suddenly dropped to her knees, hyperventilating.

The door was the obvious escape route. Being a prison door, it didn't have a lock on the inside. Instead, Dev traced his hand along the wall surrounding it, using his ability to sense the circuitry – but he could find nothing.

"The cave-in must have disconnected the power. Help me try and open it."

The three of them had trouble maintaining any grip on the smooth metal door, and with no clear indication on which way it opened, they pushed, pulled and tried to slide it – all directions at the same time, until Lot snapped at them to try each in turn.

The door remained resolutely closed.

"We're going to die in here," said Lot with a barely contained sob.

"Somebody will come," Mason said, with an uncharacteristic note of confidence.

Dev wasn't feeling so positive. He had tried his best

to ensure they couldn't be traced, and it might be weeks before the World Consortium would excavate this prison – if they would even bother, with the Collector gone.

No, thought Dev, he wouldn't accept defeat. It wasn't in him. No matter how dire the odds, he believed there was a solution. Insurmountable problems were just a list of smaller difficulties that needed to be solved in sequence.

Problem one: suffocation. They needed more air, but how could they make *air?* It wasn't as if they carried it around...

"Put your helmets on!" he commanded.

With some difficulty in the confined space, he slid his in place. After a moment's hesitation, the others did the same, and he saw the smiles of appreciation as they sucked in cool, compressed air from the suit's small oxygen canister. Dropping from forty thousand feet, where the air was too thin to breathe, meant HALO divers needed to carry oxygen. It wasn't much, but it would keep them going for at least another ten minutes.

Problem two: being buried under tonnes of earth. Once more, with just a little thought, the solution was obvious. Their PhantomSuits would allow them to scramble through the dirt as if it were water — although heading straight up would be a problem. Firstly, even standing on the floor, their ghostly feet would slowly pass through the ground and they would sink further into the earth. Pushing upwards would be impossible.

Secondly, the suit's power was designed for a single free fall. They were already running on reserve, and the notion of the power dying while they were in the middle of some other material terrified him.

The door, however...

Dev took a firm step towards the door and made as much of a practice jump as he could within the tight space, bouncing off the metal with a thud.

Lot understood what he was trying to do. "You need to get the timing right. Activate the suit the second you jump and, if you're going fast enough, you should phase through the door — just remember to cut the power before you land on the other side."

"And if I'm not going fast enough?"

Lot hesitated before answering. "You might disconnect the power before you're through the door."

"Which means I'll get stuck in the door?"

Lot pulled a grim face and nodded. "Watch me."

With little room to move, she positioned herself

against the dirt wall and used her legs to spring forward. She jumped – activated the suit – and slid through the solid door like a ghost.

Mason and Dev stared at each other in terror. They couldn't hear anything through the door, so they had no idea if Lot had made it through OK. They had no choice.

"Wish me luck," said Mason, licking his lips. Then he hurled himself towards the door, jumping – and passing through with just the slightest of noises.

Alone, Dev felt nervous. He forced himself to calm down and allowed his synaesthesia to take control of the PhantomSuit. He imitated Lot's movements exactly and made the jump.

In the corridor beyond, Dev landed on the floor with a thump as the suit powered down. He jumped to his feet and jiggled every limb to check he wasn't stuck in anything. He wasn't.

Lot and Mason, having removed their helmets, beamed at him.

"Wasn't that cool?" said Lot.

Dev shook his head. "No. I prefer using doors when they're open." He looked around the corridor they had jumped into. The klaxons were still sounding. There were state-of-the-art sensors and cameras everywhere — all of which deactivated the moment Dev was able to touch a motion sensor and use his synaesthesia to convince the system to go into sleep mode.

"This is going to be easy," he chuckled as they ran down the corridor as fast as they could. Rather than risk another phase through the second door, Dev used his abilities once again to talk to the system. The door slid open, and they entered another room with a single exit: a large freight elevator used to ship prisoners in and out.

Dev summoned the elevator and gave a reassuring thumbs up to the others. "We're going to walk right out of here."

"You know this looks bad," said Lot after a thoughtful pause. "We steal the Avro, sneak out to the prison, and the Collector breaks out the moment we arrived because you. . ."

"Led Shadow Helix straight to him," Dev finished for her.

Mason shifted nervously. "That's, um, a pretty big coincidence." He didn't look Dev straight in the eye. He glanced at Lot, who was staring at him levelly.

Dev's mouth felt dry. "I don't know how."

Lot held his gaze. "It's going to take a lot of persuading

to convince them this is a big misunderstanding. And your uncle doesn't have the largest imagination."

"You're right. Which means we can't go back."

Mason reacted in surprise, as usual several steps behind in the conversation. "Wait, what?"

"We can't return without the Collector and without Newton's Arrow. They didn't trust me before this; do you think they ever will again? And the way the Collector was talking..." Dev didn't want to finish that line of thought, but he was pretty sure that "dissolution" wasn't a good thing.

The elevator doors opened. It was difficult to say who was more surprised – the five heavily armed prison guards who had been sent to check on the prisoner, or Dev, Lot and Mason, who froze on the spot.

Then the first shot rang out.

ON THE RUN!

Mason had pulled the trigger on instinct. This time the net-gun had fired, the carbon-fibre mesh spinning out and wrapping around one of the guards, pinning his arms to his side.

His four companions raised their weapons – shock-batons, the ends of which crackled with high-voltage electricity. The batons were designed to hurt their victims and knock them out of action. Years of riot training took over, and the men surged from the elevator in a solid wall of muscle.

The elevator was the only way out. Dev knew that fleeing back the way they came would just result in their capture. The Collector's odd warning that Dev would be made *redundant* had scared him. He knew that the Collector had originally been created to look after the Inventory, just as he had. That had led to him not only escaping but also taking revenge on Charles and the World Consortium.

From an outside point of view, it now looked like history was repeating itself.

No. They had to escape in order to make everything right.

A loud crack from Lot's direction brought Dev back to the situation. She had just about managed to fend off a shock-baton using her stun gun. The loud spark had flung the baton from the guard's hand, but Lot had managed to position herself in a corner. The guards had split in a classic divide-and-conquer tactic, the other baton-wielding guard herding both Mason and Dev together in the opposite corner.

There was only one way out.

Dev shouted, "Guys, we only have one option. Use the suits."

He hoped they understood, because there was no time to explain. With a bellow, Dev charged at the guard blocking his path. The guard clearly hadn't been expecting such a blatant attack, but held out his arms so he formed a human wall across Dev.

Dev activated his PhantomSuit and jumped, hitting the guard at full speed. He was sure that what happened next would stay with him for the rest of his life. He phased through the guard.

As with the soil and door, Dev could feel the textures as he phased through the man. He thought it was like wading through strawberry jam – thick and gooey, with an unsettling taste of pork. He saw flashes of red, grey and white as he passed through internal organs, bone, flesh and fat. His ears throbbed as he heard the man's rapidly pumping heart right next to – and probably inside – his own ears. And the smell of blood was overpowering.

The grotesque nightmare was over in a second – and with a chime, Dev's suit deactivated and he tumbled into the elevator. Mason and Lot stumbled in immediately after him and sank to their knees. As the elevator doors closed, he saw the guards' horrified expressions as they pawed at their own bodies in disgust.

The elevator rose, and for several long moments nobody spoke. Then, finally, Mason broke the silence.

"I'll never eat a burger again," he said sullenly.

"We're still not out of this yet," Dev reminded him.

"We all need to stay focused now. To them, we're the enemy."

A new chime sounded in their suits, alerting them all that the power supply was about to fail. Dev shook his head in disbelief: no matter how great the gadgets, no one ever bothered to develop batteries that could work long enough.

"So we're on our own now," said Lot quietly.

Dev pulled out his phone and contacted the Avro.

"With any luck, we can slip out of here without anybody else noticing," he said in what he hoped was an enthusiastic voice.

The elevator doors slid open – and the prison's entire security force was waiting to greet them.

Without hesitation, Mason threw his hands up. "I surrender."

The guards hadn't been expecting that, and it was the perfect distraction as all eyes fell on him. Nobody was watching Dev as his thumb slid across the surface of the phone clutched in his hand.

"You two – hands up!" shouted a guard, pointing a menacing laser rifle first at Lot, then at Dev, and they both raised their hands.

"Should we get on the floor too?" suggested Dev.

The guard had been ready to bark that very order, so he was thrown, unsure what to say. Dev, Lot and Mason all dropped to their knees.

The guard took a step closer; he was feeling cocky. "Right, you miserable—"

With a roar, the guards were suddenly flung aside like skittles as a mighty downdraught of air blew from above. Dev saw that some guards who were not blown off their feet appeared to crack their heads on something invisible. They staggered, then fell alongside the others.

The Avro de-cloaked in a shimmer of air, hovering just above the ground at head height. The ramp was already open, and the teens ran for it before the guards could stop them.

Lot ran inside and headed straight for the pilot seat. Mason, who was lagging behind on the ramp, suddenly yelped as the cocky guard grabbed his leg, having scrambled up after.

"He's got me!" Mason yelled.

Dev doubled back for Mason. "Lot, get us out of here!"

Lot didn't turn around. She held the controls in both hands, and her face was screwed up in concentration.

"Gotcha!" growled the guard as he pulled Mason

back down the ramp. Mason kicked at the man's hand, but the guard refused to let go.

With a sudden lurch, the disc began to pull away from the ground; then it wobbled in the air like somebody riding a bicycle for the first time. The guard's legs dangled over the lip of the ramp as he was lifted up, then he felt himself sliding off, pulling Mason along with him.

"Help me!" Mason bellowed.

Dev grabbed a handgrip bolted to the side of the wall, his other hand snagging Mason's arm. Dev screamed with the sudden strain of supporting the weight of two people.

Below, the guards watched in astonishment as the flying saucer teetered through the air with their commanding officer hanging from the ramp. The rim of the disc caught the brick perimeter wall of the prison, denting the fuselage and causing the craft to jolt violently.

It was enough of an impact for the guard to lose his grip on Mason's leg. Mason and Dev watched as the man slid off the edge of the ramp and dropped on to several of his men below. The ramp sealed shut, and the ship shimmied, making it difficult for them to stand.

Dev managed to support himself with the back of Lot's chair before he saw the view through the cockpit canopy. They were plummeting towards the ocean!

"Pull up!" he yelled as he swung himself around the chair and slumped next to Lot.

Lot yanked the control stick backwards. They were in such a steep dive that the aircraft's belly hit the water – causing it to skip into the air.

A wave broke over the disc, causing it to shudder again, but Lot soon had the craft in a gentle climb and accelerated away from the island.

Dev patted Lot on the shoulder. "Well done!"

Lot barely acknowledged him, her brow still creased in concentration. Eventually she allowed herself to relax and looked sidelong at Dev. "So where to now?"

"Well, the World Consortium will think we've gone rogue and are helping the enemy. On the other hand, right now it looks like we might be the only ones who can stop Shadow Helix."

Lot and Mason weighed up their situation.

"When you say it like that," said Mason, "you make it sound bad."

Dev nodded. "We're on the run, guys. Fugitives."

"We'll make this work," said Lot, "won't we? And soon. My parents will go crazy if I'm not back for school."

"Of course we will," Dev assured her. He just didn't want to say that he had no idea *how*.

NO SAFE HAVEN

Charles Parker read the on-screen report for the fourth time. Sergeant Wade stood behind him, anxiously wringing her hands.

"Aliens," said Charles flatly.

"Three small figures clad in spacesuits, is what they all said. The cameras didn't record a thing. They escaped . . . in a flying saucer."

Charles Parker rubbed his temples; he was beginning to develop a migraine. "I can assure you aliens didn't help the Collector escape."

"Then who did?"

Wade had been outside of the Inventory, so Charles

couldn't blame her for not knowing all the facts. He stared at the words on the screen. He didn't want to tell her, but knew he must.

"The Avro has been stolen."

"Our Avro? Stolen?" The words were already spoken before Wade pieced it together. "And the children. . .?"

"Missing."

"I think it's a safe bet to assume they haven't been kidnapped."

Charles turned in his chair and looked at her. His face was heavy with sadness. "You are correct. Yet again, Dev tricked our security here. According to the access logs it was I who entered the hangar and took the craft on a joyride."

"But maybe they—"

"They put a guard to sleep and evaded Eema. They knew exactly what they were doing. Eema, tell the sergeant what you discovered."

Eema's voice purred over the computer. "Devon's search history indicates that he searched for the Collector's location and downloaded the navigational coordinates and the blueprints for Tartarus Prison."

Wade couldn't believe what she was hearing. "He *intentionally* rescued the Collector?"

"It appears so," replied Eema.

Wade was aghast. "I don't believe he would do such a thing."

Charles rose from his seat and rubbed his tired eyes. "It's easy to forget that the Collector himself was once a *product* here. It seems I have been foolish to ignore the behavioural patterns. As to why Dev would do such a thing. . ." He gestured helplessly with both hands.

"I told you not to trust the Collector." Wade was unable to keep the accusatory tone from her voice. "Yet you told him exactly where we were in the search for artefacts. You gave him information about Newton's Arrow he shouldn't have had!" Charles Parker looked away, ashamed. "They now know all about Professor Liu . . . because of *you*."

"I am aware of my mistakes, thank you. As it is, we must mobilize the Consortium's forces and bring them all back. That, or. . ." He paused, and then noted the shock on her face as she reacted to the unspoken threat.

"The Dissolution Protocol? You wouldn't dare."

Charles avoided her gaze. "It was created out of necessity. I don't know why Dev would go rogue – but all the evidence points to that. So as of right now, he and his friends are enemies of the Consortium."

Wade scrolled through the report and tapped the screen – leaving a fingerprint, much to Charles's dismay.

"All the cameras were out of action. But this description of the assailant with the gun outside? That sounds an awful lot like Christen Sandberg with Newton's Arrow."

"Indeed. I fear their run-in in Tokyo is the moment they may have joined forces. Devon has been acting peculiar since then."

"I don't believe that."

"Yet the facts indicate it is so."

"And this second villain. Does the description sound familiar to you?"

Charles held her gaze for a long moment before giving a curt reply. "Kardach."

Sergeant Wade gasped. "You told me—"

"What I told you was wrong." Charles turned and headed for the door. "If you find out more, notify me immediately. They need to be stopped. There can be no safe haven for them."

"Where are you going? Your nephew is out there somewhere, tied up in a business he doesn't understand."

"The Red Zone. Work does not stop." Charles stepped through the door, then paused. He levelled his gaze at Wade. "And he's not my nephew. He is my creation. You really need to put things in perspective, sergeant."

RISK
ASSESSMENT

Despite the shade, Dev was thankful for the cold drink. It was the third one he'd had in as many minutes; the Everfrost flask worked a treat. The sun blistered the ground around them, and the air was thick with heat and flies. The PhantomSuits had been oppressively hot, so he was relieved to be back in his jeans and T-shirt as he sat with Mason and Lot on the Avro's tail ramp and studied the bleak landscape.

The moment he knew they were safely away from Tartarus, he had closed his eyes and allowed his thoughts to focus on himself. The Collector had told Dev that he was been infected with a viral program to act as a homing beacon. Dev suspected that was how he had kept hearing the disembodied voice, transmitted from his own body.

Dev had used his synaesthesia to scan through his own body to detect such anomalies. It was a difficult process, as he was used to communicating with standard electronics. Bioengineering was a whole new ball game. However, he had seen the broadcasting signal; his synaesthesia had transformed it into pulses of colour and sound, and he had been able to shut it off.

He hoped they were safe, for now.

"Why here?" asked Dev, looking around at the view.

Lot shrugged. "You said go somewhere remote. I've seen pictures, and I always wanted to visit." She tapped the ramp with her knuckles. "That's what you get for giving a girl the means to travel the world."

They all took a moment to gaze at the sun peeking over the horizon, and they had to admit that it was an impressive view.

Dev had hacked the Avro's communications system, so they had all heard the reports on the Consortium's encrypted network that they were to bring in the fugitives at all costs. It had been depressing listening.

Mason spoke up for the first time since they'd fled

the prison. "I've always thought it would be cool to be a criminal on the run."

"And is it?" asked Lot.

"Nah. So far it's been a lot of sitting around and wondering what to do."

They both looked at Dev for answers. He was only half listening to the conversation, as his thoughts were on Kardach and the Collector's comments. A thought was forming in his mind, and he didn't like it. He hoped he was wrong, and that saying it aloud would mean the others would point out his mistake.

"I think I may know who Kardach is. Or I have an idea, at least."

Mason spoke without thinking. "I thought he was another... Um... Like you." He felt Lot scowling at him.

"Synthetic person?" ventured Dev, who had spent a lot of time over the past few weeks looking through the Inventory database for a suitable term.

Mason blushed and nodded. "'Cause of him saying he was your replacement and all."

Dev thought back to Tokyo and the figure in the shadows. The painful flash in his mind as he tried to deactivate Newton's Arrow. The familiar hand gestures

Kardach had performed when he silenced the alarms. It all led to one conclusion.

"He's like me, but better. With my ability, I have to touch things in order to communicate with them, to feel my way around them. I think Kardach can do it wirelessly."

"Wow, built in Wi-Fi. That'd be awesome." Again Mason felt Lot's gaze boring into him, silently warning him to shut up. "Well, it would be," he muttered.

"He's older than you," Lot pointed out.

Dev had been reading up on that too. "Uncle Parker created me and the Collector, right? That means he would have had to be a little bit older than we are now when he started. From what I found out about the Collector, evil old Uncle Parker accelerated the growing time. Which means the Collector is only really a little older than us."

Mason frowned. "Are you sure you're really our age, then?"

"Mase!" This time Lot poked her fingers into his back hard enough to make him yelp.

Dev had wondered about that himself, but avoided answering. "Back in Tokyo I felt somebody blocking my ability. I think that was Kardach."

"So he's an anti-version of you?"

Dev nodded. "The perfect defence for the Inventory if I went the way of the Collector – and now the perfect defence for Shadow Helix, wouldn't you say? If he can stop my abilities. . ."

"Then that makes you useless," finished Mason. He flinched, anticipating another poke from Lot, but it didn't happen. She was looking at Dev with concern.

Dev snorted. "Thanks, mate." He let Mason feel uncomfortable for a few seconds before continuing. "But I suppose you're right. He's protecting Newton's Arrow from being shut down. We need to take him out if we're going to stop the weapon."

"But didn't they need the weapon just to break the Collector out?"

Dev shook his head. Several steps into the future, that's how their enemy was thinking. So far the team had been lagging behind, unable to catch up. They had to do something to leap forward.

"The blue case. Whatever is in that holds the answers."

"But they have it already. We'll never know."

Dev smiled, finished off his drink and stood up. He wiped the dust from his jeans as he took in the gorgeous red and orange hues of the sun rising over Ayers Rock.

He liked Australia. It would be great to spend some time here . . . some other time.

"There is somebody who does know. And I think he may be waking up about now."

Hong Kong's sprawling harbour was filled with ships. The Avro flew low over them, an unseen ghost in the skies. A forest of huge, futuristic skyscrapers rose from the hills, covering every available space save for the wooded Peak, the highest point in the city. This meant there was very little space to land anywhere close to the city centre.

As they circled, Lot pointed to a helicopter landing pad on top of a skyscraper, then she gently put the Avro down. Dev couldn't help but admire how easily she had picked up flying the ship; she was a natural.

They emerged into the warm air, but unlike Australia the atmosphere here was thick and humid. Dev ran his hand along the hull, noticing for the first time the damage they had sustained when they'd struck the prison wall. He double-checked that the cloaking device rendered the craft totally invisible before setting the vehicle to hover high in the city, but in a space that was unlikely to have helicopters buzzing through.

*

The morning streets were already busy with lines of taxis and delivery vans clogging the city's arteries. With the swampy humidity, the teens were slick with sweat by the time they reached the address on Dev's phone.

"You're sure this is the place?" said Mason.

"This was what was listed in the Consortium's files. Professor Liu founded NiGen Labs, and he lives here. He owns the entire building, in fact."

They gazed up at the seventy-floor tower of gleaming reflective glass. Impressed, Lot whistled under her breath.

"So how do we break in?"

Dev shook his head in disbelief. "Sometimes I think you want to be a common criminal." He pushed the button on the building's intercom, both buzzing their arrival and ensuring the security camera that was linked to it stopped recording.

After a pause, a gruff voice answered. "Yes?"

"We are here to talk to Professor Liu. It's very urgent."

"No visitors. Go away."

Dev looked at the others. Mason scratched his head, gazing back up at the floors stretching skyward.

"You should have told him it was a pizza delivery. That always works in films."

Lot sighed. "At eight in the morning?"

Dev thumbed the button again, but this time he didn't wait for an answer. "Professor Liu, is that you? We are from the World Consortium, and we don't have much time. We need to talk to you about what you stored in your lab's vault in Tokyo. Particularly the blue case."

There was a pregnant pause, then the door buzzed to allow them entrance. Dev held the door open to allow his friends to enter.

"Sometimes the truth works just fine."

Their footsteps echoed through a huge marble-and-glass entrance hall that would be more at home in an international bank, yet it was completely abandoned. A glass elevator had just one button, to the penthouse floor. They ascended through sixty-eight completely empty floors. Liu was the building's sole occupant, comfirming for them all that Professor Liu was a very eccentric billionaire.

The doors opened into a massive penthouse. The large living space was decorated with pedestals bearing metal statues that looked like nothing but junk to Dev, but Liu obviously held them in high regard. A huge glass wall stretched from floor to ceiling, offering a jaw-dropping view across the city.

With a whine of electric motors, Professor Liu appeared, seated in an electric wheelchair. His face didn't look particularly old, but his body was frail. Some sort of shiny metal device was perched on one ear, extending to his temple. Dev assumed it was some sort of hearing aid, and he made a mental note to speak slowly and clearly.

If the professor was surprised at being visited by three teens, he didn't show it. When he finally spoke, it was in perfect Oxford-accented English.

"The World Consortium is recruiting younger agents each year." His eyes flashed intelligence and youth.

"Sir, my name is Dev Parker and I—"

"Devon? Ha! I have met your uncle on several occasions." The wheelchair inched closer, and Dev noticed that there were no visible controls. The old man scrutinized Dev. "So you're his nephew, eh?"

Dev swallowed, unsure how to answer. "In a manner of speaking."

Liu raised a quizzical eyebrow, then nodded. "I never much liked your uncle. Pompous, and conniving with it." He spun the chair around and moved towards the windows, beckoning them to follow. "Would you like a drink?"

Dev's "No" was drowned out by Mason and Lot's "Yes!"

Dev tensed, suddenly feeling betrayed, when he heard a familiar noise – the sound of something heavy rolling across the marble floor. He spun around just as Eema came in from a far room, the spherical orb hurtling towards them.

The robot stopped rolling. Arms, gleaming with some sort of high-tech weapon, extended from the body, and a familiar emoji head projected out. But the paint scheme on the husk was yellow, not Eema's chipped blue. The only other difference to Eema was the smooth male voice with which it addressed them.

"Apple juice, cola or tea?"

The metal arms weren't holding a weapon, but a silver tray with the offered drinks. Dev blinked in surprise. Lot burst out laughing and took the juice. Mason snatched the cola and rapped his knuckles on the robot's side.

"That tickles," said the machine.

"You remind me of somebody we know," said Mason. "Except you're much nicer."

Liu sent the robot away with a wave of his hand. His eyes were fixed on Dev, studying his reaction.

"My company designed and built them. Your Eema was once mine." He smiled at Dev's reaction. "Oh yes, we built a lot of things for your precious Inventory."

Liu circled around, quizzically regarding them each in turn. "Well, I suppose that proves you are who you say you are. Nobody with an ounce of common sense would claim to be Charles Parker's relation. You arrived sooner than I anticipated."

Dev wasn't sure what he meant, but he had no time to solve cryptic riddles. "Sir, we need to know what was in the blue case that was stolen from your lab. That seemed to be the only thing the thief was interested in."

"You are aware of what Newton's Arrow is capable of?"

Dev tried to recall some of the facts from the Inventory's database. "It uses gravitons to create gravity waves and—"

"Very good," cut in Professor Liu irritably. "You read the instruction book, bravo. No. I mean what gravity can *really* do."

"It sticks us to the planet?" said Mason uncertainly.

Professor Liu gave a dry laugh. "That's how you see it. I see it as the force that anchors us to the world beneath out feet – without it, we would be thrown out into space, to endlessly fall into the abyss of stars." He gestured above. "Gravity remains a mysterious force, even to me. It's all around us. It pulls galaxies together. I created Newton's Arrow as a unique tool, yet even I still don't fully understand it."

"How is that possible?" asked Lot.

"I merely discovered the mechanics on how to manipulate gravitons. It's as if I had constructed a canal system to channel water from a river to irrigate a field. Yet I don't know what makes water *wet*."

"That's not entirely helpful," said Dev gently.

Professor Liu raised a finger to silence him. "Being aware of one's own ignorance is sometimes more useful than knowing the limits of your understanding. What is in the blue case, you ask?"

Dev fought every instinct to tell the man to hurry. He took a deep breath and forced a smile. Eventually Professor Liu continued.

"It contains the opposite."

"Well, thank you for that," said Dev angrily. "You could have told me it contains unicorns, for all the help that is."

Dev started to turn around, but Lot grabbed his arm to stop him. "Dev! Listen to what he's saying." She smiled at Professor Liu. "I apologize for our friend. We had a rough evening last night. So, it contains the opposite... You're talking about antigravity?"

Professor Liu's face lit up, making him look even younger. "Almost!"

Dev was confused. "But we've had tech before that has antigravity. Aircraft, hoverboards..." He just about managed not to mention the Avro.

"No, you haven't. You have had technology that merely *repels* gravity. That's what antigravity does. But *negative gravity* – negravity – now, that's a different beast."

With a rumble, the not-Eema rolled into the room, his holographic head projecting concern.

"Sir! My sensors have detected a gravity fluctuation."

"What does that mean?" asked Mason, dreading the answer.

"Newton's Arrow is close by," said the professor. "As I feared, they must be coming here."

"Here?" cried Dev. "What do they need you for?"

"You said they obtained the blue case. When they opened it, they would have realized they need the red one too." The old Chinese man flashed a mischievous smile. "Rule one when dealing with people like this: always allow them the honour of underestimating you."

Dev didn't need the sermon. He had assumed they'd have a lot more time. He'd thought they would have to track the Shadow Helix posse down.

Instead they were coming to him.

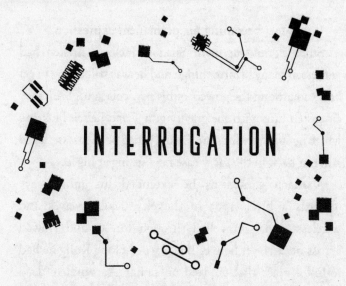

INTERROGATION

The world swirled in a halo of colours and a cacophony of sound. Kardach kept his eyes tightly closed and extended his synaesthesia further across the city. He could sense every electric cable that flashed and snapped in vivid shades. In his mind's eye, he floated through fuzzy, warm clouds of Wi-Fi signals, the huge amount of data flashing before his eyes like fireflies.

He was slowly building up a map of the city. Not one he could navigate with his eyes open, but one that told him where every device and electric signal was.

"Ah, I think I have found him," he said to Christen, who was standing behind him looking perplexed.

It was fast becoming his permanent expression.

Since signing up with Shadow Helix, Christen had witnessed many bizarre things, and he was still trying to get his head around the powers of his new colleague. Still, they entrusted him with the gravity gun — and he felt he knew where he stood with a gun. Even if it had been disassembled and put back in the carry case now sitting at his feet.

Kardach smiled as he extended his mind's eye towards a black spot in the city. Radio waves and wireless signals travelled through forests and flowed across oceans, yet here in the heart of Hong Kong he had found a place that emitted no signal. A complete dead zone, which meant it was deliberately being hidden.

Kardach opened his eyes and sprang to his feet. "It seems Professor Liu is getting sloppy in his old age."

Christen reached for the case, his thumbs already pushing against the clasps to open it.

"Not yet. This should be a simple interrogation. That's why they sent just you and me. You'll have your fun soon enough."

Kardach looked out across the city from their vantage point on the Peak's observation platform. Tourists posed for selfies in front of the skyline and paid little attention to the two men.

Then a man tapped Christen on the shoulder and, in broken English, asked if Christen minded taking a picture of the man and his wife with the harbour in the background.

The South African gangster was unsure what to do; people rarely treated him *normally* any more. But Kardach gave him a wary nod, indicating he should just do it to blend in. Christen took several photos, each with his thumb clumsily obscuring the lens, before he followed Kardach to the funicular, which would take them back down into the city, towards their prey.

Dev pleaded with Professor Liu. "We have to run. You don't know how bad these people are."

"I have known worse, Dev. Besides, I am too old to run or spin my wheels." He laughed at his own joke, then gestured around. "This was always going to be my final palace of solitude. Of course, I never wanted it to turn out this way. Breaking new frontiers of technology should be an exhilarating ride of discovery. Instead ... other people used my creations for the wrong reasons. I turned my back on NiGen Labs, just keeping a watchful eye over them, to make sure they didn't stray outside the moral guidelines I had set."

His frail body managed to look even weaker as he slouched under the weight of memories and regret. He stopped moving altogether.

For a second, Dev thought he had died. He exchanged an alarmed look with Lot. She coughed politely – and Professor Liu suddenly sprang back into action. He whirled his chair to face Dev.

"I created several safeguards. That's why there are two cases. You should go and find the red box."

"Go where?"

Professor Liu smiled as he adjusted a control on his "hearing aid" – the chrome clip that wrapped around his ear and pressed against his temple. Dev felt his head spin – and then he suddenly knew where the case was.

"The power of the mind," said Professor Liu, tapping the device. "A wholly intriguing area of research."

"But I still don't know what's in the cases."

"You will know, when the time is right."

Mason flinched as the door buzzer sounded. Everybody looked at one another, unsure what to do. Eventually, Liu used a small control pad on the side of his wheelchair to answer.

"Yes?"

There was a pause, then a hopeful voice. "Pizza?"

Mason wagged his finger at Dev. "See? *That's* how it's done!"

Dev shuffled anxiously from one foot to the other; he recognized Kardach's voice. "We have to leave now."

Professor Liu shook his head. "No. *You* have to leave now. Now that you share my knowledge, you are just as useful to them as I am." Mason and Lot exchanged bewildered glances.

Dev hesitated – long enough for the elevator to ping as the car descended to the lobby. The bad guys were in the building.

Lot pulled Dev aside. "Dev, if they have Newton's Arrow with them, this is the closest we've been. We could take it, and end all this right now."

Kardach tried to sense what lay ahead, but his gifts were still drawing a blank. He was helped by Christen, who stood behind him, assembling the Newton's Arrow and humming a tune to himself as if it were his very own action soundtrack.

"Do you mind?" snapped Kardach.

The theme tune died on Christen's lips. He hoisted up the complete gravity gun and activated the power. Almost immediately it began to increase in mass – and for a second Kardach was worried that the elevator car would slow down and they wouldn't make it to the top floor.

But his fears were unfounded. With a soft *bing*, the doors opened and he was suddenly swamped by a rush of colours and sound that buzzed around his mind's eye and drew his attention straight towards Professor Liu, sitting in his wheelchair with his boulder-like robot behind. The friendly emoji head was now a fierce scowl, the serving arms replaced with glowing energy cannons.

With a single wave of his hand, Kardach wirelessly infiltrated the robot's circuits and deactivated it. The holographic head spluttered – the eyes briefly replaced with crosses before it faded. The cannons instantly powered down and the spherical hulk rolled across the floor like a discarded ball, until it gently bumped to a halt against the wall.

"Professor Liu, there was no need for such an aggressive reception. I merely want some information from you."

The old Chinese man tilted his head defiantly. "You are unworthy to receive it. Whoever you are."

Christen raised the gravity gun menacingly. Instead of being intimidated, Professor Liu laughed. "And what am I supposed to do? Plead for my life? I am too old for that. Do your worst."

Kardach looked at Christen and raised his eyebrows. This wasn't going to be as easy as he'd hoped. Kardach puffed his cheeks and exhaled a long sigh.

"OK. Have it your way."

The electric motor on Professor Liu's wheelchair suddenly whined to life with such ferocity that the wheels spun before gaining traction on the smooth floor. The old man was propelled backwards, almost falling out on to the floor. The wheelchair struck the panoramic window with great force, sending massive cracks zigzagging across the surface of the glass.

Enjoying the show, Christen carefully lowered Newton's Arrow to the floor. It had grown too heavy to hold comfortably. He stretched his back and flexed his arm to get some sensation back.

"Still not ready to talk?"

Professor Liu sneered. Before he could reply, Kardach shot the chair forward, then violently back again, an action so severe that Liu was tossed around like a rag doll.

The wheelchair struck the window once more, and this time it shattered. Huge shards of glass sheared off and fell to the street below. Professor Liu's chair stopped, the back wheel precariously balanced on the edge. A strong wind blew in from the shattered window.

Kardach took a menacing step forward. With a simple gesture, he made the chair tilt backwards – then forward just before it could fall.

"You're making life so difficult for yourself," he teased.

Professor Liu just smiled. "Kill me and you don't get any answers. I wonder what your boss would think of that?"

Christen was about to volunteer to extract the information, but he only got as far as opening his mouth before something whacked him across the back of the head. He stumbled to his knees and, as he lost consciousness, saw Dev standing over him wielding one of the heavy metal sculptures.

At the sound of the scuffle, Kardach spun around in time to see Dev hoist up the Newton's Arrow – which took every ounce of strength he possessed.

Dev took great pleasure in the surprised expression on the villain's face. "This is the end," he wheezed. He had hoped to sound like an action-movie hero, but the weight of the gun had taken his breath.

Kardach smiled, pitying Dev. "No. This is the beginning." With one mental gesture the wheelchair's motor squealed — and Professor Liu shot backwards through the window.

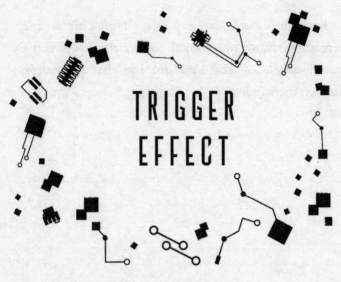

TRIGGER EFFECT

Dev didn't think. He just acted on instinct. His synaesthesia told the weapon exactly what he wanted to achieve – and he pulled the trigger before Kardach could stop him.

Energy streamers lashed out around Professor Liu's wheelchair as he soared a metre away from the window and towards certain doom. The energy formed a bubble around the chair, suspending it high above the ground. The safety bubble even remained when Kardach extended his hand, palm out, towards Newton's Arrow.

Dev was the only one who saw a huge flash and felt as if pins were pushing into his skull as Kardach's wireless powers conflicted directly with his synaesthesia — almost overriding his senses.

Howling in pain, Dev dropped the weapon. It thudded against the marble, shattering several tiles. Dev dropped to his knees, clutching his head.

Kardach advanced towards him. "I am surprised. I thought you and your little cohorts had all been buried alive. Not that it matters. When will you learn? You're looking at Mark Two, right here, the second generation of *you*. I am superior in *every* way."

"Not in every way," said Mason, emerging from a side room. Kardach hadn't been expecting that. "For one, you talk way more than he does."

"And Dev has better hair," said Lot, stepping from a room on the other side, brandishing one of the more pointy sculptures in Liu's collection.

Mason placed both hands on the robot husk, which was taller than he was, ready to push. Kardach extended his hand towards him, firing his synaesthesia power.

"Um, what is that supposed to do?" sniggered Mason. "Or are you just planning on breaking my watch?" He glanced at his watch. It had stopped. "You git!" he roared, and used all his weight to launch the defunct robot at Kardach.

The metal boulder rolled straight for him. Kardach threw himself over a couch, overturning it in his haste to escape. The robot rolled straight past and shattered another panel of glass as it plummeted to the street below.

Mason grimaced, imagining the damage that was going to cause. "I was always rubbish at bowling."

Lot slashed the sculpture through the air in a menacing manner; several of its protruding blades glinted in the light, the sharp edges giving Kardach no doubt that it would hurt or even kill him. "I, on the other hand, have always been very good at hitting my targets."

Kardach took a few steps back, then raised his hands in a show of surrender. "OK, OK. You've got me."

Dev stood, feeling woozy as he rubbed his head. His attention was drawn to Professor Liu, who was still floating outside, his arms waving frantically. The professor was being carried further away by the wind.

"Professor Liu!" Dev realized then that Liu wasn't just trying to get his attention; he was pointing. He turned and saw Christen holding Newton's Arrow. Dev made a mental note: next time, hit the bad guy over the head harder.

With a leer, Christen aimed the weapon at Dev.

"I'm gonna enjoy this."

"Go ahead!" Kardach shouted. "I've unblocked it!"

The weapon hummed to life — but Christen's mocking laughter was quickly cut short when the weapon made a peculiar crackling sound.

The orb suspended under the barrel — the graviton pod, Dev recalled from his brief communication with the weapon — glowed from within, as before. But now there was also light seeping through a widening crack in the casing. The damage must have been sustained when he'd dropped the weapon and Dev could now see a kaleidoscope of swirling particles inside, pivoting around a miniature black hole.

"It's going into overload!" Kardach exclaimed in horror.

Christen replied with a scream that became a brief gurgle as his entire body stretched like strands of spaghetti — and he was sucked into the centimetre-wide crack.

With no Christen to hold the gun, it dropped to the floor for a second time. This time the pod split in two with a bass heavy boom that rattled Dev's fillings.

An opaque energy orb shot out from the broken graviton pod — first in one direction towards the shattered window, before the pod peeled apart, spilling gravitons in every direction — and with it utter chaos followed.

Dev felt himself falling. The wind was knocked out of him as he crashed to the floor. Confused, he looked around to get his bearings – he was lying on the *ceiling*. Kardach was lying on one vertical wall, while Lot was lying on another, perpendicular to Kardach. Mason was almost annoyed to realize he was the only one standing normally on the floor.

Every window in the building had exploded from the pressure of the gravity wave – and each particle had fallen in its own direction. Up, down, sideways – forming a cloud of spinning glass shards.

The entire skyscraper groaned as every surface took on its own gravity – some walls and floors strained as they pulled together; others were repelled as gravity was scrambled.

Dev noticed the gun still on the floor – or rather, from his perspective, the ceiling. It was still activated, churning out even more gravitons. He strained to reach for it – but couldn't.

"Kardach! Turn it off or it'll kill us all!"

Kardach was no fool. He knew this was no time to fight. He strained to extend his power … but nothing happened.

"I can't! The gravity field must be disrupting my signal!"

"I'll do it!" yelled Mason. He ran for the gun.

"Mase, no!" Dev warned, but it was too late.

Mason vaulted over the couch — and found himself suddenly falling *up* to the ceiling, where he landed with a thud next to Dev. Disoriented, he looked around. "That wasn't supposed to happen."

Lot's gaze met with Kardach's. Their eyes narrowed — and they both sprinted for the gun, running on opposite walls around the apartment.

"Don't go near it," Dev cautioned, fearing Lot would suffer the same fate as Christen.

But she wasn't listening. There was a ninety-degree corner ahead of her. Gritting her teeth, she made the leap. Incredibly, she soared through the two gravity fields and landed on the new section of wall. She was so surprised that the move worked, she stumbled to her knees, buying Kardach more time to perform a similar move on to the opposite end of the very same wall, bringing him closer to the malfunctioning gun.

Dev crossed to Mason, noticing that amongst the debris cast across the ceiling was Liu's telepathic ear clip. It must have fallen off Liu when he was hurled out of the window, Dev thought. He pocketed it and nudged Mason with his foot. "Give me a boost up ... down ... whatever."

Mason rose unsteadily, inverted as he was on the ceiling. Dev placed his foot in Mason's cupped hand. "Ready?"

"GO!" yelled Dev.

Mason heaved the same moment Dev jumped. It was the ultimate boost. Dev sailed into the centre of the room. Without changing direction, he felt his stomach twist as he came under the influence of the floor's opposite gravity field. It was as if he were on a high-speed roller coaster. Mid-fall, Dev flipped over and landed perfectly on the real floor. He lunged for Newton's Arrow—

At the same time, Kardach leapt from the wall and arced face-first to the floor as the rules of gravity switched around him. He landed unceremoniously on a smoked-glass coffee table, which shattered under his weight. He blindly reached out and touched the weapon the exact moment Dev did the same.

Their duel synaesthesia power soared through the device, both commanding the weapon to shut down. Everything happened in milliseconds, although in the world of enhanced vision, Dev experienced it as if time had slowed.

Their combined powers sent an overload of

instructions surging through the weapon – causing it to turn off and on in a furious series of rapid pulses. With each wave, the reaction in the fractured graviton pod was pushed closer to critical mass.

Dev yanked his hand away from the gun the moment the graviton pod exploded, spewing a mighty *gravityquake*.

It was like being hit by a soft inflatable wall that expanded – and showed no signs of stopping. Dev and half the furniture were thrust through another window, which exploded around him. The shattered particles of glass flowed outwards with him rather than falling to the ground dozens of storeys below – and Dev reflected that he was yet again having to endure his fear of heights. No, it was no longer a fear – it was a hatred. Mason cartwheeled next to him, moving wildly out of control.

The two boys were carried in a straight line – towards another building. Again windows imploded as the gravity wave struck, a second before Dev, Mason and a ton of junk were carried through. Still their journey did not stop. Desks, internal walls and support columns all ripped away as the wave continued. Office employees were swept up and carried with them – yet nobody was struck by the millions of pieces of debris floating around them, being deflected from one another in their own private gravity fields. Everything seemed to be gently orbiting something else, like a dizzying array of miniature solar systems.

As they crashed out of the side of the building, Dev was spun around as if he were floating in the current of a river. He looked back at the skyscraper they had passed through, and couldn't believe his eyes. It was splitting apart in *every* direction, and doing it in a slow ballet. Professor Liu's building beyond had been similarly torn into several chunks that were dispersing across the city and colliding with other tall buildings, which broke apart in turn. The entire penthouse they had been standing in was still almost intact as it spun lazily skyward.

Dev suddenly felt branches whipping at his face; he and Mason were hitting the forested slopes of the peak. The duo, now out of the graviton influence, crashed to the sharply inclined earth with bone-jarring thuds. The office workers swept up in the wave were similarly cast through the trees. They, too, looked back at the bewildering spectacle behind them.

A circular chunk of the city had been hit by the

gravityquake. The centre point of devastation was a mass of particles floating and spinning in zero G.

Further out from this dense mass, the destruction of buildings lessened. Instead, entire skyscrapers had been plucked up and were lazily spinning through the air. Dev could see people still inside, pounding the windows in panic as they gently rotated. Numerous vehicles drifted past, some with drivers still behind the wheel as they soared upside-down fifty metres above the ground, occasionally being deflected from one another, wrapped in their own gravitational comfort blankets.

As the gravityquake's effects ebbed away, it was business as usual in the rest of the city, beyond the blast zone.

Mason laid a hand on Dev's shoulder. "Mate, I think we just broke Hong Kong. I reckon we get out of here as soon as possible and *never* mention we were ever here."

Dev nodded, then looked around. He felt a growing sense of panic.

"Mason . . . where the heck is Lot?"

DISSOLUTION
PROTOCOL

Getting out of Hong Kong was tricky. With the destruction still floating in place, it was clear that gravity wasn't going to return to normal any time soon. Every street was gridlocked, every pavement crammed with people filming on their phones. The likelihood of finding Lot or Professor Liu in the chaos was remote at best.

Instead Dev and Mason clambered back up the Peak, and Dev used his phone to summon the Avro. They were able to board unseen and hover over the city.

"She'd call us if she could," Mason pointed out.

Dev knew that, and the fact that she hadn't made him feel sick.

"Maybe she's, y'know, d—"

"Don't say it!" snapped Dev. He had always believed that problems could be overcome by breaking them down into smaller tasks. From tracking down the jetpack thieves to breaking into the Collector's prison. However, Lot being dead . . . that was a problem that couldn't be overcome.

"So what are we going to do?" asked Mason, his head in his hands. "We don't leave a man behind, right? Or a girl," he added with a weak smile.

"We might have to," muttered Dev.

"Dev, no—"

Dev looked up, feeling sick as he spoke. "If she's alive, she's smart enough to find help. If she's dead. . ." He couldn't continue. He focused back on the controls and instructed the Avro's sensors to search for Newton's Arrow. It drew a blank.

"Nothing?" In frustration, he slammed his fists against the controls. Dev wondered if the mass gravity fluxes were interfering with the sensors. Did the graviton orb destroy the weapon, or did Kardach manage to grab it and slip away?

"Looking for the gun is more important than looking for Lot?"

Dev looked up. "If Kardach got away with Newton's Arrow, then we can't waste time here. More lives are at stake."

"Finding Lot is *not* a waste of time," Mason snapped. "We aren't leaving without her." He pushed Dev aside and switched to the disc's camera system, which was capable of reading the fine print on a crisp packet from forty thousand feet. Using the simple touchscreen, he programmed Lot's image into the computer and let it run facial recognition on the millions of people below. If she was there, it would get a hit. Eventually.

Dev nudged him. "Mason."

Mason didn't look up. "Give me a minute."

"MASE!" This time Dev held Mason's jaw and forced him to look up.

The Avro's viewport was filled by a military helicopter directly facing them. The port's on-screen graphics helpfully identified it as a CAIC Z-10 attack helicopter and went on to point out the thirty-millimetre cannon. With a wholly inappropriate thumbs-up icon, it also confirmed that the HJ-10 missiles under the stubby wings were locked on them. The only thing the perky computer hadn't highlighted was the slack-jawed look on the pilot's face.

"How can they see us?"

Dev looked back at the camera feed on the monitor and saw that lots of people were looking directly up at them. He touched the control bank and closed his eyes in order to communicate with the system.

"The cloaking device is busted," he said, remembering the damage they'd sustained from the prison escape. Now that he could sense the ebb and flow of the Avro's systems, it was clear the damage was in the area that housed the stealth technology. The gravity wave must have been the final straw for its delicate electronics.

"Maybe you're right. Maybe we shouldn't hang around," said Mason.

Dev didn't need to be told twice. He accelerated the disc as fast as he could, away from Hong Kong and out over the open ocean. He just hoped that Lot was safe, wherever she was.

A chill passed through Lot's body, shuddering her awake. Opening her eyes felt like more effort than it was worth because when she did, everything was blurry.

The last thing she remembered was seeing Dev and Kardach dive for Newton's Arrow. There was a piercing scream – she wasn't sure whose – then a blast of energy that sent her weightlessly spinning. She caught a fleeting glimpse of Mason, flailing as he soared away from her at speed. Then something hit her head and she blacked out.

She tried to scratch an annoying itch on her chin, but her hand didn't move. Was she paralysed? She fought the urge to panic and instead took a deep breath and waited for her vision to clear.

Little by little, the room around her came into sharp relief. And it wasn't a familiar one. It was white, mostly, save the occasional flakes of rust that indicated the walls were metal. A deep hum resonated through the chair she sat in, vibrating her bones. No, not sat in, was *strapped* in. Her hands and feet were bound with crude Velcro straps, which was why she was unable to move.

Prisoner. The word rattled through her mind, and again she fought the urge to panic. The question was, a prisoner of whom? The Hong Kong police? The World Consortium? Or Shadow Helix?

She called out. "Hello?" She strained to listen for a reply, for any sign of movement. "Hell-o-o!" she said louder. "This is your friendly prisoner here who would like very much to go the toilet!" She didn't need to, but thought it was as good a way of gaining attention as any other.

At the top of her lungs, she began to sing a new chart song she'd heard recently on the radio. She didn't know all the lyrics, so she filled in the blanks with the rudest words she knew. With the little movement she had, she stomped her feet on the floor for added effect. They gave a dull thud that sounded almost hollow.

After several long moments the door opened and a cloaked, hunched figure appeared, dragging its right foot behind as it entered. She could hear raspy breathing from beneath the hood.

"Stop singing!" the figure yelled, and a deformed, slender hand reached up to pull away the hood.

Lot stopped straight away. She couldn't take her eyes off the hideous creature beneath the hood. She also couldn't stop herself from screaming.

Charles Parker couldn't pull his eyes away from the numerous monitors on the bunker wall, all showing the same thing: news footage of a flying saucer hovering over a half-destroyed Hong Kong. He knew exactly what had happened, but he found little mirth in listening to international reports talking about an alien invasion.

"How did they find Professor Liu?" Charles demanded.

197

Eema spoke over the computer system. "Apparently Devon is more resourceful than you gave him credit for. He took the files before he left. Unless you are referring to Shadow Helix — in which case, I believe you yourself gave the Collector everything he needed."

"Oh, go and delete yourself!" snapped Charles.

"I am unable to comply."

"Is there any sign of Liu?"

"I have searched hospital records and found no trace of Professor Liu."

"We need to know what he told Devon. What if he told him the location of the second case? *We* were never told its location. Can you trace the Avro?"

"I am unable to do so. It was last seen heading due east over the Pacific Ocean. Satellite recon has detected nothing, and they are not transmitting any flight data. We will only find them if they show up on camera or if the public reports another sighting."

"Then they're as good as invisible. They won't make the same mistake twice." He rubbed his chin thoughtfully.

"Charles, the Consortium is demanding answers. This is the biggest tech disaster to date."

Since its formation, the World Consortium had

worked with governments and the United Nations in keeping history-changing inventions a secret. The explosion over Tunguska, Siberia in June 1908 was seen across most of northern hemisphere. It was blamed on a meteor strike, rather than the experimental antimatter engine that a Russian scientist was testing. The 2012 blackout in India, which affected six hundred and twenty million people, was in fact caused by a small gizmo that was designed to deflect rain over cities, to prevent flooding. These and many more inventions were deemed either too unstable or vulnerable to be used for *completely* wrong, and deadly, other purposes. The public was kept in the dark to prevent both general panic and further research into areas of science that should be left alone.

In every instance they had been able to cover up the real causes. But now, with worldwide media showing a UFO hovering over a localized gravity distortion, facts couldn't be concealed. But Charles knew the *truth* could. As unpalatable as it sounded, he was going to have to allow the public to think this was an act of alien sabotage.

"What are we to do about Devon?" said Eema.

"Do you really think he has gone rogue?"

"His rap sheet now includes assaulting several Consortium guards, stealing technology, freeing a prisoner, evading capture, possibly assassinating Professor Liu and most definitely destroying Hong Kong. If these are not deliberate acts, then he must be the clumsiest person in the world. Why else would he do this?"

Charles sighed. He had been trying to work that out himself. "I don't know what goes on inside the boy's mind; it's the one place I can't see."

"I think it's time to activate the Dissolution Protocol." When Charles didn't respond, she prompted him again. "I said, it's time to activate the Dissolution Protocol."

He nodded grimly. His eyes scanned across the screens one last time. He was gravely disappointed that yet another one of his projects had gone so wrong ... and this time he felt a pang of something unfamiliar: sorrow.

FOLLOW MY LEADER

"Time is against us," said Dev, after thoughtful consideration. "And going back to search for Lot is not going to be quick or easy." He held Mason's gaze. "We have to continue on."

Mason nodded, but his jaw clenched. "Just so we're clear. If I go missing, then you wouldn't come back and look for me either?"

"It would depend on the circumstances. But, well, no. I wouldn't. Just like now."

"Well, at least I know where I stand."

"Good."

"Good."

Tension grew in the silence that followed. Dev concentrated on flying the Avro, a task that Lot was much better at. Finally Mason broke the silence.

"If I'd twisted my ankle and was slowing us down—"

"Get ready for landing," Dev cut in, determined to blank him.

Mason peered out of the viewport. In the distance the horizon was filled with imposing mountains, but below there was nothing but an unremarkable patchwork of fields dusted with snow. Dev steered away from an airfield, and they landed with a bone-jarring bump in a clearing amid a copse of fir trees.

They set about gathering fallen branches and tossing them on to the Avro in an attempt to camouflage the craft, now that the cloaking device was broken. It wasn't working very well, and it soon started to snow. Mason blew into his hands to fend off the cold; he wasn't dressed for the biting chill.

"Where are we?"

"Échenevex," Dev said.

Mason gave him a blank look.

"France," he added.

Mason looked around at the empty fields doubtfully. "And Professor Liu hid the case in, like, a bank vault around here? He certainly picked someplace random."

Dev couldn't elaborate on the details of the telepathic imprint he had received from Professor Liu. He had just suddenly *known* the information, like digging up an old memory. It was as if the memory had been downloaded into his head, and he just had to "remember" it. That meant he didn't know what lay ahead, exactly, and he didn't know if there was more to "remember". He just had to go with what he knew and hope he'd be able to come up with more information as he went along.

He absently patted his pocket to check that Professor Liu's telepathic ear clip was still there. Sure enough, it was, next to the translator he had put there when the battery had started to fade.

"It's not in a bank vault, exactly."

"Then where? In a gigantic hole? Ooh, or maybe inside a massive baguette?" said Mason.

Dev tried to recall the foreign memory. "I think it's more of a time capsule." He sounded puzzled by his own statement.

They studied their attempt at hiding the Avro. It was pretty appalling, but they hoped it would throw off the casual passer-by. Not that anyone was likely to be walking by here.

Dev hauled the kitbag over his shoulder. "Let's go."

It was a short walk through the trees before they reached a field of cows. The animals didn't look pleased to be out in the snow, and Dev tried to ignore their suspicious bovine stares as the boys climbed the wooden fence.

A group of buildings lay ahead. They could see a large sign on the side of one of the buildings. Dev stopped as he suddenly "remembered" in greater detail where Professor Liu's time capsule was buried. But if Professor Liu had a plan on how to retrieve the case, he hadn't shared it with Dev.

"CERN?" said Mason with a frown as he read the sign. "Why does that sound familiar?"

Dev knelt to rummage through his kitbag. "It's a scientific research place. Here, clip this on."

Mason looked at the round pin-badge Dev had handed him. There was no picture on the front, just a series of curved lines engraved into the metal surface, which reflected a hue of colours when angled in the light.

"What is it?"

"A BlurBadge."

Dev called up the Inventory catalogue entry, the display hovering over his watch. It was a copy of an old instruction paper, written in a font that must have seemed futuristic in the 1980s.

Fool your friends with the BlurBadge! Strap it on and nobody will know who you are! Your friends' muddled brains will fill in the blanks. Why not rob a bank today?

"I can see why it was banned," said Mason.

"Yeah. Things were weird in the eighties. When we get inside, just act confident, as if we belong in there."

Mason pinned the badge on – a tricky manoeuvre with his cold, large fingers – and looked back at the sign on the building. "Hold on. Isn't this the place with the Large Haggis Collider?"

"Large *Hadron* Collider," Dev corrected him. He saw the look of panic cross Mason's face.

"Isn't that the thing that people are worried will destroy the world?'

Dev shrugged and zipped the kitbag back up. "I hope not. But then again, knowing our luck. . ."

He activated his BlurBadge and trudged across

the field towards the main gates, Mason reluctantly following behind.

Théo had been a guard at CERN for three decades. He loved working at this facility. It was here that the internet was birthed, the existence of the Higgs-Boson particle confirmed and other reality-shaking discoveries were still being made. He knew every one of the two thousand, two hundred members of staff – or their first names, at least.

So when two short men approached the gates, he wondered why he couldn't recall their names, and why he was starting to get a headache.

He put his phone down and rubbed his suddenly tired eyes. He squinted at the men as they drew closer. They were complete blurs, although, oddly, everything around them was in focus. He hoped he wasn't coming down with something; there always seemed to be at least one illness going around.

As the newcomers drew closer, their faces seemed to shift into vaguely recognizable ones – but even those seemed to alter from one person to another. The men held up ID badges as they walked past and smiled, both offering a cheery *"Bonjour"* in terrible French accents.

"Good morning, Mr ... er ... and Mr ... um..." stuttered Théo, feeling a flush of embarrassment for forgetting their names.

As Mr Er and Mr Um casually walked into the complex, Théo sat back down and rubbed his eyes again. The terrible headache suddenly vanished as quickly as it had come. He'd have a baguette for lunch, he decided, not realizing how much Mr Um would approve of that decision.

"Wow," breathed Mason as they walked out of view of the guard, behind one of the buildings, and stopped at a large statue. It was difficult to look at each other with their BlurBadges activated, but very slowly their features came into sharp relief for both.

"Um, Dev..."

"I know." Dev took his badge off. Just by touch his power notified him it needed recharging. "Well, at least they got us this far."

"That was weird. I really didn't think it would work. He looked at us as if he knew us!" Mason looked at the old fast food loyalty card he had used as an ID. The BlurBadge had made it unreadable while the security guard's brain had filled in the required details. "Knew this would come in handy one day! Two more stamps and I get a free cheeseburger too."

Dev frowned at the statue looming over them. He didn't know what it was, but Liu's memory of it surfaced. It was a dancing image of the four-armed Hindu deity Shiva. "The cosmic dance of creation and destruction. . ." whispered Dev. He noticed Mason's odd look. "Just something I was remembering."

Mason looked around. "So which building is this thing in?"

Dev knew it was here, somewhere. It was just the details that evaded him. . .

Then it came to him. A slow awareness as the memory pushed through his mental fog. He looked down at his feet.

"We have to dig for it?" asked Mason, following his gaze.

"Sort of," said Dev.

One hundred and fifty metres below their feet was the collider tunnel. A massive circle, twenty-seven kilometres in circumference, and the place where particles were smashed together at almost the speed of light.

And that's where he remembered Professor Liu had hidden the case.

STRANGE TIMES

In the end, Lot was left to scream until her dry throat went hoarse. Then she sat in embarrassed silence when it became apparent that the crooked figure before her hadn't made any move to harm her.

She looked a little more carefully at the man's hands. One was normal, but the right one was too thin; the fingers were twice as long as they should be. The same problem continued down that side of his body. The foot that looked as if it had been run through a mangle; the chin and entire side of the head that was prised away from the skull, making it look as if a crescent moon had collided with his face, leaving the left-hand side normal and completely recognizable.

"K-Kardach? What happened?"

Kardach's harsh breathing quickened for a moment. "The graviton leakage did this to me." He touched his warped face. "A split second is all it took."

Lot recalled how Christen had been sucked into the miniature black hole at the centre of the Newton's Arrow graviton pod. For him, it was all over in the blink of an eye; for Kardach, she could see the pain on his face with every movement he made.

"I'm sorry," she said in a low voice. She meant it too. He may be the enemy, but her father had taught her to respect people, even those who meant her harm. She just hoped that he felt the same.

Kardach scowled as if the thought of sympathy was a physical strike across his twisted cheek. He wheezed, dragging his foot as he limped closer.

"You have been summoned." He unfastened the straps binding her to the chair and indicated to the door.

"What? No handcuffs?" said Lot in surprise.

Kardach growled, or it may have been a laugh. Lot tried not to smile. Obviously he didn't think she would put up much of a fight. What a terrible mistake for him, she thought as she was led down the metal-walled corridor.

They reached an elevator and headed up. By the time they arrived, Lot's suspicions about her location were confirmed.

The elevator doors opened on to the bridge of a cargo freighter. Massive windows offered a view across a calm, blue ocean. The deck of the ship itself extended out the length of several soccer pitches, and it was bare, save for dozens of lifeboats hanging over the edges, suspended on winches.

Two uniformed crewmen on the bridge didn't look away from their instruments as Kardach and Lot entered.

"This is Shadow Helix's base?" said Lot.

A voice chuckled from the far end of the bridge. "This? No, child. Merely a transport that will take us to our destination."

Lot turned to the speaker. He was an average-sized man, with unremarkable looks, the kind of person who would blend in in any crowd. When Lot glanced to Kardach and back, she was aware that she'd already forgotten what he looked like. He was memorable for being utterly forgettable.

"Please forgive us for tying you up, but you have a track record of being difficult. Drink?"

Lot shook her head. Once again she glanced at Kardach. She marvelled that he seemed to actually be afraid of this unassuming man.

"You must be Double Helix?"

The man laughed, waving his hand as if swatting the comment aside. "A name created by others to instil a certain fear within people. But it will suffice."

"I take it you are not planning to release me."

"No."

"But you think that I will help you?"

"Will you?" he asked in surprise.

"No."

"I thought not," he said pleasantly. "All that's really important is that you are safe and well, because when the time comes, your friends will do anything to keep it so. *Anything.*" The last word dripped with such malevolence that it sent a shiver through Lot. It left no doubt in her mind that the villain's ultimate plan didn't include her safe delivery home.

NOT SO
TOTAL RECALL

"It always looks easy in the movies," Mason grumbled as he clawed his way through the air-conditioning tunnel that he was convinced was getting even more constricted.

Breaking into the air-conditioning building had been stupidly easy once Dev had looped the security camera feeds and put the intruder alarms to sleep. Crawling down the air conduits had been Mason's idea, and Dev couldn't think of anything better – air needed to be circulated underground, and that's how they usually did it in films.

However, Dev was slowly learning that the big screen

was not a useful guide, as films tended to gloss over awkward situations – such as Mason barely fitting in the tube. He was forced to leave their precious kitbag on the surface. And now they had reached a junction with the options of going left, right, straight on – or dropping one hundred metres down.

"Down's where we're supposed to go," said Dev. Fortunately it was a black hole, and the light from his mobile phone barely illuminated anything, so he wasn't feeling his usual waves of vertigo.

"Could do with a rope," Mason said aloud. "I should make that invention, a rope in a bag."

"We're going to have to do this the old-fashioned way."

Mason was alarmed. "You mean dropping straight down?"

Dev sighed. "No, like, climbing down. Arms and legs stretched like this." He demonstrated, holding them straight out. "Brace your back against the wall, and slowly shuffle down."

Mason was reluctant, but agreed they had little choice but to slowly clamber down the shaft. Their damp trainers squeaked on the metal, constantly threatening to send them plummeting. Dev regretted going first, as every time he stopped Mason would continue until his bum knocked Dev's head – threatening to dislodge him.

After what seemed like an endless journey, they finally reached the bottom of the shaft. Dev had assumed the tunnel would sensibly bend at the bottom and come out in a wall. Instead it ended with a fan below them, heavy blades rapidly scything the air.

"See," said Mason, peering down. "If we had fallen, we wouldn't have been splattered on the floor. We would have been sliced and diced by that."

Dev reached for the fan's central motor. All he had to do was touch it to establish contact with the circuits beneath and shut it down. A simple act ... if only he could reach. Dev's fingers groped the air just above the metal housing.

He clenched his fist and concentrated, wondering if he, like Kardach, could wirelessly transmit his powers. He strained, his arm shaking, the veins on his forehead pulsing ... yet nothing happened.

He was forced to edge lower down the tube, closer to the whirling blades. The strong breeze ruffled his clothing, and he could even feel the air moving through his jeans, giving him goosebumps. He stretched for the motor again...

It was still beyond his grasp.

"Dev, stop messing around."

"I can't reach it!" He flinched at the sound of wet rubber screeching on metal. "What was that?"

Mason sounded calm but strained. "I'm losing my grip. Now would be a good time to hurry."

Dev glanced up to see Mason slip a few centimetres closer. Mason's legs were trembling with exertion, pushing against the side of the tube, but his trainers continued to slowly slide.

Dev readjusted his position. Any lower and he would be sitting on the blades. He bent forward and stretched for the motor housing between his legs. His fingernails touched the surface – but it still wasn't enough contact for his synaesthesia.

Another drawn-out squeak from above – and Dev suddenly felt the pressure from Mason's backside on his shoulders.

"Mason!"

"My feet are going!"

The added weight painfully folded Dev's body over – but it was enough to force his hand on to the engine mount, and more importantly a wire that ran along the edge. That was all the contact he required to use his synaesthesia. He commanded the fan to perform an emergency stop. The motor died, the blade rapidly slowing down.

Dev breathed a sigh of relief.

Then Mason's grip gave way and his full weight fell on to Dev. There was no way Dev could support them both. He dropped on to the blade – now thankfully rotating more slowly – and their combined weight sheared the supporting bolts.

Dev, Mason and the entire fan fell through the ceiling and into the collider tunnel below.

Pain jolted through Dev as they landed on a huge blue pipe running down the centre of the tunnel. He bounced off the pipe and crashed to the floor, parts of the broken fan motor strewn all around him. For a moment he lay face down on the cold concrete floor ... and groaned.

"Dev? Are you alive?" hissed Mason.

Dev's pain left him with little doubt that he was, indeed, alive. He pushed the fan off him and slowly stood up. They were in a well-lit long tunnel that gently curved in both directions. The blue pipe he had rebounded off was about the same width as the air-conditioning tube, and it ran the entire length, in the middle of the floor, with alternating coloured sections of blue and silver.

Dev "remembered" the tube was the collider itself, and — because yellow warning lights were flashing and a klaxon was whooping — another of Professor Liu's memories surfaced, telling Dev that the alarms meant the accelerator was powering up, and particles were already rushing in a beam around the tunnel thanks to powerful magnets.

A collision was about to take place.

Professor Liu hadn't supplied any additional information about how bad it would be for them to be in the tunnel during a collision, but as the experiments were designed to rip atoms apart to see inside them, Dev concluded that it must be bad.

He pulled himself to his feet, then realized he was using the accelerator pipe to do so. He immediately let go, wondering what would happen if he linked his synaesthesia to a particle accelerator. Again, it probably wasn't a sensible thing to do.

Mason was already on his feet and looking around with wide eyes. "Every time I'm in a tunnel with you something *bad* always seems to happen." The memories of being trapped in a vacuum tunnel were still very fresh in both their minds.

"This way," said Dev. "I remember it's close by."

Mason hurried after him. "Do you realize how weird that sounds?"

"Lately, weird seems to be the default setting of my life."

They didn't have to jog very far to reach the part of the collider that looked familiar to Dev. A triangular warning sign was etched in the side of the tube, featuring the World Consortium logo. The scientists here assumed the engineers had placed the symbol here, and the engineers ignored it, thinking the scientists needed it to calibrate their experiments. Like a lot of Consortium affairs, Professor Liu's "time capsule" was hidden in plain sight.

If being one hundred metres below the earth in a particle collider could be considered "plain".

The bottom of the arrow pointed straight down, signposting exactly where Professor Liu had stowed it: behind a metal panel.

A countdown in French began over the public address system. Dev pressed against the indicated panel. It didn't budge. He pressed harder, and still the panel remained where it was. That was when he noticed it had been screwed into place. Professor Liu's memory of it didn't include screws. Dev guessed the panel may have fallen away over the years, only to be screwed into place by a helpful technician.

"I need a screwdriver."

Mason patted his pockets. "I don't have one. I must have left it in my other jacket," he said sarcastically. "Typical. We have access to the coolest gadgets in the world, but then we really just need a screwdriver, and we don't have one."

With a grunt of annoyance, he pushed Dev aside and began kicking the panel. It buckled, but held. He continued, his face twisting into an angry snarl as he took out his frustrations against the metal.

The countdown continued. Dev regretted not paying any attention during French lessons, as he had no idea how long they had left. Then he remembered the translator still in his pocket. Mason had lost his in Hong Kong, while Dev had taken it out to save the fading battery. He inserted it into his ear, activated it – and his heart sank, despite the flawed translation:

"Two minutes to *baguette*. . ."

COLLISION COURSE

BAM! The countdown was continuing, but at least Mason had finally booted the metal panel off. There was a hollow recess behind it, perfectly formed to hold the red case.

"Bingo!" said Dev, sliding the case out. There were no visible clasps or hinges, just a narrow line around the edge indicating where it opened. It felt empty too, but he had no time to ponder. "Got it! Now let's get out of here!"

They both stood, but then froze as a nearby door in the side of the tunnel opened. Three armed troops, clad in matt-black armour and fearsome masks that covered their faces and mouths, ran into the tunnel and swept their rifles around – and quickly found their two targets.

Meanwhile, the countdown continued unabated. Dev realized that the troops had not announced their arrival to the scientists in the control room on the surface, and his looping of the cameras would leave the scientists unaware of what was happening below.

Sergeant Wade emerged from the open door. "Dev. Put the case down and give yourselves up. I must bring you in. For your own sake."

"We've been set up," replied Dev, glancing around for any chance to escape. The only available direction was further down the tunnel. It would hardly be a thrilling chase, and all Wade had to do was stay where she was, since they would eventually run in a circle.

"Are you saying you didn't release the Collector?"

Dev hesitated. "No! We were there . . . but Kardach and Christen Sandberg broke in and freed him. And you know about Kardach, don't you? You should. He's just like me. Another secret in the Inventory that Charles decided to keep to himself?"

Anguish crossed Wade's face. "You've got it wrong, Dev."

"So he wasn't created as my replacement?"

"He was," Wade admitted. "But your uncle created him under direct orders of the Consortium. He was against it. He felt that you were perfect. They wanted to push the experiment further, to cut out the emotions that make you. . ."

Dev found the word she was floundering upon: "Human?"

"Your uncle won the argument, and the project was suspended. Kardach was placed in suspended animation, deep storage for the living. Until he was taken from the Red Zone, just like everything else in there. Shadow Helix's facilities spurred his growth to make him mature and develop, even beyond your abilities. You see, Dev, Charles was on your side. It was Double Helix who took an abandoned project and brought it to life."

The story rang true, but Dev didn't know what to believe. "But I heard you. I heard what you both said about not trusting me." Either the sergeant was a terrific actor, or the confusion on her face was genuine. "You were driving my uncle in the Jeep?" he prompted.

"No . . . that's what spurred you to run away? We were talking about the Collector. Your uncle was trusting him too much, showing him Inventory files so that he could help work out what Double Helix was after. That's how they knew where Professor Liu was; your uncle had inadvertently given them everything they needed." She pointed to the case. "Except this."

Dev wanted to believe her. More than anything, he wanted to believe his uncle was prone to human mistakes too. The raid on the Inventory had been successful in terms of stealing artefacts, but Shadow Helix had been unable to prise information from Eema's systems. It had taken his uncle's foolishness to give them that.

"That means the Collector intended to be captured all along," Dev said in a low voice. Double Helix really had planned ahead.

"You can see how bad this looks?" said Wade. "You steal the Avro. You're there when one of the most notorious criminals in history is sprung from jail. Then you go on the run, help destroy Hong Kong, and then break in here."

"Are you crazy?" snapped Mason. "We've been set up; we've just said so!"

"If that is all true, then what about Lottie?"

"You know where she is?" said Dev with relief.

Wade's brow furrowed. "Of course. She's with Shadow Helix." Her confusion grew when Dev and Mason exchanged worried looks. "But you knew that?"

"She's a hostage!"

Wade shook her head in disbelief. "Dev, we intercepted radio communications saying she had switched sides voluntarily. Just like you both had."

"No! That's what they want you to think. If the World Consortium is busy chasing us, they can do what they're planning without interference. Why else would they send such a message, knowing you would intercept it?" He saw the indecision on Wade's face. Dev's knuckles went white as he gripped the case. "They want this. That's why they have her — they expect a trade."

"If that were true . . . you know we can't risk such an exchange. There is no way we can allow Double Helix to get his hands on that. We'll put it somewhere safe."

"Like the Inventory? He's already raided it once. And then what do we do about Lot? Just forget her? Put her into 'deep storage'?" His words were heavy with sarcasm. "Do you know what's in the cases?" Wade shook her head.

Dev and Mason took a step backwards, prompting the four troopers to adjust the aim of their rifles.

"I want to believe you, Dev. But you must understand, from where I'm standing, it looks as if you've got yourselves involved with the wrong side. Do the right thing now."

Dev sighed and placed the case gently on the ground. Mason looked at him in alarm.

"Mate, what're you doing? That's the only way we're gonna be able to get Lot back!"

Dev leaned on the collider tunnel with both hands spread out in surrender. He met Mason's gaze. "I'm doing the right thing. Like I always do."

The colours that flashed before Dev's eyes would blind anybody, but in his mind's eye there were no retinas or delicate eyeballs to sear. Instead the entire, monstrous LHC came to life in a string of ultra-complex machinery that stretched all around, below and above him – from the collider itself to the sensors to the massive computer systems controlling it all. In the blink of an eye he saw that there were other tunnels, branching off into smaller loops – he was tracing the electronic systems of the largest single machine in the world. It gave him an instant migraine. It reminded him of the one time he had tried to use his synaesthesia on the internet and quickly disconnected himself, fearing that his head would explode.

Except this time he wasn't going to disconnect.

He was going to turn the collider into a weapon. Fortunately, Professor Liu's memories did include handy details on how the LHC worked. All it took was for Dev to affect a few of the super-magnets that accelerated atomic particles around the tunnel, altering their power just a little as the countdown reached zero.

The protons were slipped into the collider in opposite directions, travelling a shade slower than the speed of light as they followed a beam no more than a millimetre wide. Because the protons were so small, millions of them would pass head-to-head without ever crashing into one another. Powerful magnets reduced the beam's width, forcing the protons to collide and unleash colossal amounts of energy. The very same magnets Dev had tampered with. He just hoped he'd affected them by the precise amount needed.

He grabbed Mason around the collar with both hands and pulled him to the floor—

—at the exact moment billions of protons deflected from the magnets, just like a snooker ball off a cushion, and rebounded through the collider wall. Even at high speeds, a single proton wouldn't do too much damage – it would be like being pricked by a pin.

But a billion of them. They punctured through

the side of the collider in an intense stream of light that sprayed across the gap between the troopers and Dev. The energy stream tore across the concrete walls, blasting them apart.

The Troopers threw themselves backwards to avoid the stream – piling on top of Wade and knocking the breath out of her.

Seconds later the scientists in the control room on the surface reacted to the barrage of danger alarms and shut the collider down. The beam instantly stopped ... and there was no sign of Dev, Mason or the case.

THE DISSOLUTION PROTOCOL

Charles Parker entered a room he seldom visited. The Inventory was peppered with many such locations, but this particular place gave him no joy to be in.

It was a spherical chamber built with just one purpose in mind: the control of Inventory assets.

"Eema, call up file alpha-four-six-eight."

Pictures of Dev appeared on the screens, taken from birth through to just a few months ago. Every aspect of his life, from minor colds through to his especially crafted abilities, appeared in finely detailed reports. Dev was never mentioned by name, just by the cold term *biological asset*, which was given to any of the Inventory's artificially created living creatures.

Charles read through it, but his gaze kept sliding to the pictures of Dev, and his heart sank. He had always attempted to keep a distance between his own feelings and his experiments. It something that he had failed to do with the Collector, which was why he had trusted him. Charles wanted – needed – to believe that their connection, their history, meant something.

After the Collector's initial escape from the Inventory, Charles had been instructed to make a fail-safe device that would mean no other biological asset could ever escape and turn on its creators.

Unlike the Collector, or even Kardach, he had not accelerated Dev's growth, meaning the boy had had a regular upbringing. Try as he might, Charles had attempted to stay emotionally distant, but it had been almost impossible. Every night he tucked Dev in bed he had tried to remind himself he wasn't a real boy, he was just a biological asset. A fake.

A fake with a personality. That began to make Charles question exactly what it was to be human. When he started work on Kardach he vowed to speed-grow the asset and not engage with its personality at all.

But Dev had been different. In many ways the prototype of what Kardach would become, but he also had his own unique abilities too. And within him Charles and Eema had together created the Dissolution Protocol as the final backstop should things go wrong. He had considered activating Kardach's, but the assets were too precious to wantonly destroy, and the evidence against him was nowhere near as damning as the catalogue of destruction following Dev. Charles tapped the screen, calling up the Protocol activation screen. Through the combination of a sixteen-digit passcode, he traced a complicated pattern across the screen, enabling him to access the system. The panel on the control desk before him liquefied, the metal morphing into a new batch of controls.

"Protocol sequence activated," said Eema's disembodied voice.

Reluctantly, Charles places his palm on a smooth metal plate. He felt a series of pinpricks as it took samples of his DNA. When creating Dev he had started by using parts of himself – his very own DNA. They were more closely related than Dev realized.

"Target match confirmed," purred Eema without any emotion. "Do you wish to activate?"

Again, Charles hesitated. Once triggered, there was no going back. The device would send out a low-frequency signal that would trigger a biological self-destruct switch that was built into Dev. He would literally melt apart from the inside out. Terminated.

The World Consortium had warned Charles that one more mistake would end the asset's usefulness, and Dev's actions had added up to several major mistakes.

"Activate the trigger pulse," whispered Charles, the words barely forming on his lips.

The screens before him tinged red to indicate the process was under way. They didn't have to, but the whizz-kid software programmer at the World Consortium who wrote the code had a flair for the dramatic.

"Dissolution Protocol activated," said Eema. Then, as if sensing Charles's delicate emotional state, she added, "Would you like me to get you a cup of tea?" Then, "There is an incoming transmission from Sergeant Wade."

"On screen," commanded Charles.

Wade appeared on-screen, the surface buildings of CERN behind her. "They found the case and then escaped through a service tunnel. Oh, and they've broken the Large Hadron Collider." She waited for Charles's volcanic reply, but instead he just gravely bowed his head.

Wade continued. "Dev insisted that they have been set up, and that Lot was being held against her will. They're planning to use the case to negotiate for her release. If you want my opinion, I believe them."

Charles's gaze bore into the machine in front of him. What if she was right? He had activated the Protocol already. He had just signed Dev's death warrant. And there was no taking it back.

A CASE
OF NEED

Mason strained to open the case as he balanced it on the side of the Avro's control panel. In his struggles he managed to knock the two recharging BlurBadges to the floor and slam the case against his thumbnail, which then started to turn black, but still failed to open the case. He shook it, but couldn't hear anything move inside.

"Will you stop that?" said Dev. "You could blow us up! Or break something on the Avro, and I don't fancy hitch-hiking around the planet."

Mason froze; that hadn't occurred to him. Since they had fled from CERN and had taken flight in the Avro, he had been attempting to prise the case open. He gently placed it on the floor and they both stared at it.

Mason was the first to break the silence. "You still don't have any idea what's inside this, or inside the blue one?"

"Liu said negative gravity, but I have the feeling that's not the whole answer."

Mason shook his head. "Whatever it is, it's something so important that they've torn up three cities to get it. So it isn't money. But . . . what?"

The Collector's words echoed in Dev's mind – Double Helix was always several steps ahead. Something troubled him. "What if we're looking at this all wrong? To get the first case, he used Newton's Arrow."

Mason gave him blank look.

"But he didn't need it, did he? He could've found another way of breaking in," said Dev. "He stole a ton of stuff from the Inventory, but it's Newton's Arrow that he's chosen to use to go after these cases. What if the cases and the gravity gun are linked somehow?"

Mason shrugged. "I'm more bothered about how we use this to get Lot back. Are we really gonna hand it over? It doesn't feel right."

Dev looked at him in surprise. "Wait a minute, what happened to all this *you can't leave a man behind* rubbish?"

"That was when you actually did! It's different now that we know she's safe—"

"Safe? She's a hostage!" Dev nearly shouted.

Mason looked down, saying nothing.

"This isn't the time to be thinking about double-crossing Double Helix. Let's free her first, and then worry about how to get it back. If we don't manage to get it back, well, the World Consortium might believe our story at the very least."

Dev knew that he was being used by Double Helix, and he hated it, but he could see no other way of rescuing Lot.

"So how are we supposed to find him to do the exchange?" Mason finally asked.

"I wouldn't worry about that. He'll know we have it by now. He'll contact us."

"What? Like, by text?" said Mason, glancing at his phone – noticing for the first time there was a text on it. He bolted upright in his seat. "Hey! It's from Lot!" He held up the message for Dev to see. It was a string of numbers. "Mean anything to you?"

Dev had seen something like them before. He typed the numbers into the Avro's computer system. The screen turned blue.

"Uhh ... did you just break the screen?"

It took a moment for Dev to work out what they were looking at. "No. These are longitude and latitude coordinates. Look, it's the ocean. The Pacific."

He zoomed the map out until he could see the closest land mass, Australia – and that was still pretty far.

"At least there won't be any innocent people around to get hurt this time."

"And no place to hide in the open water," said Dev ominously. Still they had no choice but to follow the trail.

And if they were going to survive the encounter, Dev thought, then they were going to play their enemy at his own game. "We'll need backup."

Mason wagged his phone and said sarcastically, "Shall I just text Sergeant Wade and tell her?"

"Yes." Mason waited for the punchline, but Dev was serious. "We're going to be there in half an hour. This might be the last chance we have to call for help."

Mason nodded and punched in a text to Wade's number.

Dev noticed the troubled look on his face. "What's the matter?"

It took Mason several moments to find the words.

His thumb hovered over the phone entry marked "Home". "When you said this could be the last chance, just now... I just wondered what my parents would think if I didn't return home. Or Lot's parents ... if something happened to us."

The idea that Lot and Mason had lives of their own, with parents and siblings, holidays and silly traditions – Dev hadn't really appreciated that until now. With no family of his own, he could only imagine what was going on in their minds. It occurred to him that with loving homes to return to, they had a lot more to lose than he did. Perhaps that was exactly what Charles Parker was trying to protect him from? A life that was simple and uncluttered; one with no emotional attachments or responsibilities to others made life easier ... and very lonely. Dev didn't have any answers, and he had even less time to have a heart-to-heart with Mason.

"Don't think about it." It was a callous thing to say, he knew, but he really needed Mason to keep his focus. "Mason, nothing bad is going to happen. Trust me. We're going to walk away from this – Lot, too – and it'll all go back to normal. Or at least as normal as Inventory life can be."

That's all the assurance Mason needed to hear. He forced a smile and slipped the phone into his pocket. Then he looked at Dev and frowned.

"Hey, why is your nose bleeding?"

Charles was alone in the Inventory command bunker. The screens were still playing news reports about Hong Kong, and the "alien attack" was being wildly speculated about by so-called experts. It was all laughable, but Charles had blocked out the media feed; his eyes were unfocused, thinking about his time in the Inventory and how the last few months had turned the place upside down.

Perhaps it was time to retire, he mused. Could he really put up with any more emotional roller-coaster rides?

"Incoming transmission from Sergeant Wade," said Eema. When Charles didn't stir, she spoke up again. "I detect from your body functions that you are neither sleeping nor dead, Charles. I said you have an incoming—"

"Remind me to check the programming in your sarcasm module," he cut in. "Put it on-screen."

He couldn't bring himself to look at the image of

Wade. "Charles, we have been sent GPS coordinates from Mason. They're for a location in the Pacific Ocean."

Charles steepled his fingers across his nose. "Why would the lad have sent that information to you?"

"It's either a trap to lure us in, or it could be the rendezvous with Double Helix. Depending on which side they're really on."

The options swirled around Charles's head. "Eema, cancel the Dissolution Protocol."

"You know I cannot do that. You designed it as an enclosed system. There is no off button. The trigger pulse has already been sent."

It was a low-frequency pulse that would take a little time to travel the globe, but it would eventually reach its target. Charles closed his eyes. It was now just a matter of time before Dev was terminally shut down.

"Charles?" Wade's voice dragged him out of his malaise. "What should we do?"

What should *he* do? Charles stood and paced the room. He always thought best on his feet. The pulse had been sent, but in theory it could take *days* to activate. The Protocol had never been tested; its effects were undocumented.

Then a thought struck him. *Biological asset ...* there was another solution.

"Wade. Deploy every naval asset the Consortium has and head to the location immediately. Find Dev and bring him back home."

THE ART OF ESCAPE

Lot adored roller coasters, aeroplanes and any kind of turbulence, yet the slow, rhythmic rise and fall of the boat made her stomach churn and her legs shake. Her knuckles were white from clinging to the ship's steel gunwale.

Despite the ship's motion, the weather was calm and she could see clearly to the horizon in every direction.

"What's going on?" she asked Kardach, who was keeping close by as he watched grey-clad Shadow Helix technicians prepare the raised helicopter landing pad located amidships. "There's nothing out here!"

"Not yet. But there soon will be," Kardach assured her. "Have you heard of the legend of Atlantis?"

Lot's eyes widened as she looked back out across the ocean. "Are you telling me there's a sunken city down there?"

"Not quite, but . . . you'll see."

"I hate to tell you this, but I need the bathroom." Kardach shot her a suspicious look. "Seriously this time. Look, even evil master plans need to include a few toilet breaks."

Kardach indicated she should follow him, and he started walking towards the bridge tower towards the stern. After several steps he noticed Lot wasn't following him. She stood with her arms stubbornly crossed.

"I think you can get one of your hench-*ladies* to show me where it is."

With an irritated snarl, Kardach called to one of the grey-suited technicians. Close up, Lot saw the technician was a pretty young woman with her hair tied in a ponytail.

"Show the prisoner to the bathroom and don't let her out of your sight."

The woman nodded, drew a small taser from her belt, then indicated Lot should walk in front.

"And get her back here as soon as possible!" Kardach snapped as they walked away.

Lot allowed her minder to guide her to a bathroom on the deck level of the command tower. She went through the motions in the toilet while the guard stood outside the stall.

Lot flushed the toilet, then crossed to the sink and filled the basin. She splashed her face, allowing the cool water to soothe the motion sickness.

"Hurry up," growled the girl, who, despite her delicate looks, had a voice that could melt lead.

"I'm not feeling too good," said Lot, stalling for time as she filled her cupped hands with water and splashed her face again.

Impatient, the guard, taser still in one hand, strode over and grabbed Lot's elbow. That was what Lot was hoping for. She moved with startling speed and spun around, her elbow slamming down on the girl's hand so hard she heard it break.

But the guard was no shrinking violet. She thrust the taser at Lot – who was still spinning and able to deflect the weapon by striking the girl's wrist with the open palm of her hand.

Lot was filled with so much adrenaline that everything seemed to happen in a slow-motion ballet. Off balance, the guard couldn't stop plunging the taser into the sink. Lot darted backwards as the falling woman's motion caused her finger to pull the trigger, and several thousand volts exploded in the water as she shocked herself unconscious.

The woman dropped like a sack. Lot didn't waste any time in dragging her into the stall and then using the woman's belt to bind her legs and hands to the pipework. She then ensured the guard was tightly gagged with a cloth towel hanging from the basins, so she wouldn't be able to raise the alarm when she regained consciousness.

Only then did Lot search her. There was an ID card that probably worked as a key card too. From the LED display, the taser still held a decent charge. Lot pocketed it.

She considered disguising herself with the guard's uniform and escaping into the bowels of the ship, but it would only be a matter of time before she was found, and with nowhere to go in any direction she had little choice but to play the role of prisoner.

But with a taser and an ID card, she had a hidden advantage. She retraced her steps to the deck. Kardach didn't notice her until she was by his side. He didn't comment on the guard's whereabouts; why should he?

She had returned, so he assumed the guard had simply gone back to her duties on the deck.

Lot followed Kardach's gaze skyward as the Avro, looking scratched and battered, slowly descended through the few fluffy clouds above. Lot was thankful she had returned on time; this could be her one chance off this ship. She rubbed her cold hands, then put them in her jacket pockets – her fingers resting on the taser tucked inside.

Dev had broken into a sweat. Trying to keep the Avro hovering over the moving freighter was tough enough, especially as a brisk wind was blowing from the side, continually forcing him to correct his course. As a result, the aircraft wobbled in every direction. Hardly the imposing entrance he'd hoped to make.

Plus he was feeling nauseous. He'd managed to stem the nosebleed with his sleeve, but it had been replaced with a headache and an uneasy sensation in the pit of his stomach. Now wasn't the time to be coming down with the flu.

Mason pointed at the screen. "There's Lot!"

Dev gritted his teeth and nodded. He was relieved to see her, but he had to keep all his attention on flying.

Every landing he'd made so far had been bumpy, and that was on to solid, non-moving earth. Attempting to get the Avro on the helipad would be challenging, to say the least.

"What is that thing with her?" exclaimed Mason in disgust. "Looks like some kind of monster. . ." He trailed off as they drew closer. "It's Kardach! Wow. . . Look at his face!"

Desperate not to be distracted despite Mason's outbursts, Dev bit his lip as the deck inched closer. The aircraft swayed over the helipad like some kind of drunkard.

Mason's narration continued as he studied the dozens of identically suited Shadow Helix cronies below. "None of them look armed. In fact, I don't see any weapons on deck at all."

"They don't want to scare us off," said Dev slowly as the helipad wobbled beneath them. "But I bet you a million quid there are at least a dozen weapons trained on us right now." The Avro's threat detection system hadn't picked anything up, but Dev assumed that was one of the many broken things on the aircraft.

"You don't have a million quid," Mason said, then shot him a quizzical look. "Do you?"

The landing was so hard that Dev thought he'd dented the helipad. Certainly the sound of *something* cracking echoed through the ship. On-screen he saw Lot grimace in sympathy and, next to him, Mason spat out a filling.

"Look what you did!" he said, holding it up.

Dev closed his eyes as the room rotated around him. He pulled himself together and saw Mason regarding him with concern.

"I'm all right," he said dismissively. "Are you ready for this?"

Mason studied the viewport. Dozens of hostile faces watching the craft expectantly. The bleak ocean around them. And Lot, standing expressionless – an indication that she had something up her sleeve.

Mason stood up and picked the red case off the floor. "Let's get her back."

PRISONER
EXCHANGE

Lot hoped that the Avro was still airworthy after Dev had dropped it to the deck with such force that one of the helipad steel supporting struts buckled, sending a resonating boom through the ship.

As the disc's ramp lowered, she saw Kardach tense. She couldn't see any weapons amongst the assembled Shadow Helix personnel. They all stood to attention, arms by their sides. Even Kardach was unarmed.

She looked up at the ship's bridge, seven storeys above them. It was difficult to tell, with the sunlight glinting off the glass, but she was sure there was somebody standing there. She reasoned that if she were Double Helix, that's where she'd be.

Her attention was drawn back to the Avro by movement from within. Dev slowly descended the ramp, wearing his kitbag and clutching a red case. She heard a low, triumphant exhalation from Kardach.

Dev's gaze met Lot's, and, to her complete surprise, she suddenly heard his voice whispering in her head as if he were standing just behind her shoulder.

"Lot – it's me, and no, you're not going bonkers." She surreptitiously looked around, expecting another Dev to mysteriously appear behind her. "I'm using Professor Liu's TelePath so only you can hear me."

"Bring the case forward," Kardach commanded.

Dev looked Kardach up and down, making his disgust apparent. "You got real ugly, real quick."

Kardach ignored his insult. "The case for the girl!"

"Lot for the case. She comes over here first."

Kardach scoffed. "Ha! Do you think I was born yesterday?"

"Well, that's the thing, you sort of were, and I think it's obvious that Uncle Parker really didn't make them the way he used to."

"You are testing my patience, boy." He grabbed

Lot around the neck. His clammy, extra-long fingers encircled her throat, causing her to yelp.

Dev quickly stepped off the ramp and placed the case down on the floor. Then he took a step backwards.

Lot was on Kardach's un-deformed side, and she could see indecision on the half of Kardach's face capable of displaying emotion. He pushed Lot forward and walked behind her, using her as a human shield.

"Get ready to run," rang Dev's voice in her mind as she drew nearer to him. Her fingers tightened around the taser in her pocket.

A voice suddenly shouted out. "Before you do anything, Devon, are you not curious to know what is in the cases you have risked your life for?" A door had opened up at the bottom of the bridge tower, and Double Helix strode out holding the blue case.

"My friends are more important," Dev shouted back.

"Ah, noble sentiments." He drew next to Lot and Kardach and placed the case down at his feet.

Lot's gaze was drawn to the blue case. It was within easy reach. All she had to do was make a break from Kardach, snatch it and ... somehow get on the Avro before anybody could react. She became aware that Double Helix was looking at her with a half smile.

"I wouldn't do that if I were you." His lips didn't move, and with a gasp the question formed in her mind: *You can read my mind?*

Helix's thin smile was all the confirmation she needed. She looked urgently at Dev – had his thoughts been intercepted? Was *his* mind being read?

Helix turned his attention back to Dev. "Let's be reasonable. You know I was never going to allow you to simply" – he flicked his fingers through the air – "fly away with everything I had so diligently worked for."

Before Dev could react, enormous metal claws snapped from the deck, reached into the air and clutched the Avro's rim, holding it in place like a giant mousetrap. Double Helix's laugh echoed across the ship.

Then Dev suddenly sank to his knees, blood trickling from his nose. Lot saw the flicker of a puzzled frown cross Double Helix's face. Mason ran down the ramp to support Dev.

"Now, there is no need for violence," Double Helix said. "And there is even less need to dawdle. Mason, bring the case to me."

Mason scowled and made no move.

Helix let out a long sigh. "Bring the case to me, or her neck will snap like a twig."

On cue, Lot felt Kardach's long fingers tighten, and she couldn't breathe. She let go of the stun gun and used both hands to claw at his gnarled fingers. Mason angrily picked up the case and carried it over. Helix held out his hand – but Mason stubbornly dropped it, smirking when he saw Kardach flinch.

Kardach shoved Lot towards Mason and snatched the case up, checking it for signs of damage. Satisfied, he nodded at Helix.

Lot and Mason retreated to Dev's side. He was still hunched on the Avro's ramp, trying to stop his nose from bleeding.

"What happened to you?" Lot asked.

"I don't know. I'm coming down with something, I think."

"It's not an illness, Devon," said Double Helix as he supervised a technician carrying both cases to a lifeboat at the edge of the ship. "You are suffering from a fail-safe mechanism triggered by Charles Parker. The Dissolution Protocol, he calls it. Think of it as an auto-destruct."

"Help him!" Lot pleaded.

"There is nothing I can do. The Protocol was Charles Parker's insidious invention, not mine." He studied Dev for a moment. "It's a shame. I could have used you and your abilities in my organization."

Kardach ran his finger along the seam of the blue case. It unfolded open with a hiss. Inside, both halves were filled with a blue lattice structure made of fine, delicate-looking threads, like candyfloss.

He carefully placed the open case in a special metal slot on the boat, then turned to the red case and repeated the proceedings. Again, inside was a lattice structure, but a red one. Kardach placed it in the slot next to the blue case.

"You may have thought the case was empty," Helix explained. "But what you are looking at are intense negravity fields. Just as a magnet has two poles, north and south, so does a gravity field, to ensure it all flows the same way. Your flying disc defies gravity in the same way magnets will repel each other if you push the same poles together. That's antigravity. However, these negravity fields are essentially a world of their own. Observe."

He turned to watch the lifeboat as it was lowered into the water by a small crane. There was more movement as the Collector came on to the deck through a bulkhead door, Newton's Arrow slung over his back. He cast Dev a brief glance before joining Double Helix's side.

"It's one big family reunion for the ugly squad," muttered Mason.

"Let me see," said Dev, struggling to stand. He leaned on Lot's shoulder, and they all watched as the remotely controlled lifeboat zipped across the ocean, away from the freighter.

Double Helix didn't look away from the boat. "Look what happens when you expand a negravity field."

The Collector held out Newton's Arrow to Kardach. "After what it did to you, I have no wish to fire it."

Kardach reluctantly took the weapon, noticing that everybody took a wary step back from him as he flicked the switch to activate it. He took aim at the receding boat. As the gun powered up he was forced to spread his feet to take the increasing weight. Then, he fired.

It was the strongest gravity wave they had yet witnessed. It arced over the ocean and struck the boat. Even from far away, they could see the two lattices in the cases absorb the graviton stream like a sponge.

For several seconds nothing happened, and the stream continued. Then the lattices rapidly expanded, bleeding into each other in a bright magenta flash that forced everybody, except the Collector, to shield their eyes.

As Lot's vision came back, she could see that the

water around the lifeboat had become a frothing maelstrom. The lattices were rapidly expanding – unfolding like Slinky springs, but performing moves that seemed to defy logic as they blended into each other.

Against all logic, the lattices continued expanding with a growing rumble. The larger they grew, the more familiar the shapes they formed. Towers began to stretch into the air, and Lot realized that – incredibly – they were watching *an entire city* unfold before their very eyes.

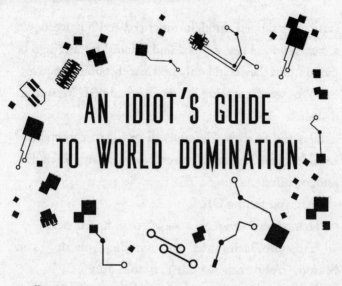

AN IDIOT'S GUIDE
TO WORLD DOMINATION

A floating cityscape spread across the horizon, a vertical wall of grey steel buildings that blotted out the sun and bathed the ship in deep shadow. The sudden creation sent huge waves crashing towards the freighter, causing it to violently bob and roll. As the last section of towers expanded into position, the thunderous rumble gradually faded away. The incredible expansion was over in less than a minute. The entire city, roughly several miles across, had unfolded from the two cases.

With everybody's attention on the spectacle before them, Dev grabbed the kitbag and pulled Lot and Mason towards the nearest bulkhead door. Using her stolen key card, they slipped through unnoticed and hurried down a passageway. They stopped and listened for any sign of pursuit, but they could only hear the throbbing engine.

"We were carrying a *city*," exclaimed Mason in disbelief.

Dev didn't reply. He was still trying to comprehend Double Helix's words. He only looked up when Lot nudged him.

"Are you feeling OK?"

He nodded, although it wasn't true: he felt sick.

"I'm sure Helix was just winding you up," said Mason. "Your uncle wouldn't try to . . . um. . ."

"Kill me?" said Dev bluntly. "That's exactly the kind of thing he'd do." He wanted to feel angry about it, but could only drum up acceptance of the fact that his uncle had triggered a self-destruct. Could he blame him? All the evidence pointed to Dev working for the other side; he had played into Double Helix's hands time and time again. And now, finally, he had delivered the case to the villain, giving him everything he needed.

Dev chased the morose thoughts from his mind. If things were going to end, then it would be on his terms. He would at least prove his innocence and bring Double Helix and his whole operation down with him.

"So, this city," Dev said. "Crushed down by gravity." He was trying to replay events in his mind, searching for Double Helix's motives. "The *only* way he could have expanded that city was with Newton's Arrow. Professor Liu had said the weapon was unique."

"Which meant Shadow Helix had to break into the Inventory to get it. And that's all he really wanted?"

"Maybe he took everything else as a bonus? But that means whatever is in the city is more valuable that anything we have. Had," he corrected himself.

The fact they hadn't yet been chased and that no alarm had sounded indicated that either their disappearance hadn't been noticed, or that Double Helix didn't see them as a meaningful threat; that seemed more likely to Dev.

They heard a dull clang. Then the entire ship trembled and the engines fell silent.

"I think we've docked with the city," said Lot. She looked at Dev with concern. "If you're not well, we should go. Leave this for Sergeant Wade to deal with."

"I don't want to run," said Dev, drawing himself to his full height. He felt more resolved than ever, determined to use Helix's own arrogance to defeat him.

*

The Collector couldn't help but be impressed as he looked up at the city. He knew the mechanics behind it, that it had been shrunk down to hide it from detection; that during the process, half the city had been charged with negravity and stored in the red case, while the blue case contained the *regular* gravity component. Mixed together . . . it was quantum cookery.

He understood that the negative gravity fields in the cases had kept both halves weightless and protected. Only when the intense stream of gravitons from Newton's Arrow had vaporized the negravity had it allowed the two halves of the city to merge back together. The gravitons had then expanded it back to its full size.

The scope of the quantum physics behind it sent a chill tickling his spine as he walked down the freighter's gangplank and set foot in the cold, quiet streets. It was a ghost city, and he, Double Helix and Kardach were the only occupants.

Double Helix led the way, with Kardach carrying Newton's Arrow *just in case*, and the Collector bringing up the rear. The rest of the crew remained on the freighter; a few units had been ordered to find the problematic children.

The footsteps of the small expedition team echoed eerily in the streets; the only other sound was the wind whistling between the high tower-block spires.

The Collector wondered what kind of warped mind had designed such a city, bringing a nightmare into the real world: the building facades were angular, some with jagged projections poking from the sides like crowns of thorns. Some structures had bridges connecting them high above, while the streets themselves had no pavements, road markings or foliage. In fact, the entire colour scheme was limited to dark grey or black. In the shadows the construction material soaked up light like a sponge. Everything was jagged and grim.

"What is this place?" whispered Kardach.

"A PocketCity," the Collector replied in a low voice. "Did you ever consider what happened to those secret bases and island lairs the bad guys of old used to use? Professor Liu worked with the Inventory on a rather novel way of hiding them, by increasing their density and shrinking them to a tiny size, like a white dwarf star."

"All of this was inside those two cases?"

Kardach nodded towards the buildings. "Why not destroy it all?"

"Fortunately for us, Professor Liu was a savvy businessman. Why destroy technology when he could make money from it? That was his deal with the World Consortium. He would make their devices, and in return he would be allowed to exploit certain technologies for a profit. That is why he kept the cases himself rather than in the Inventory, and they kept Newton's Arrow. One needed the other, a perfect arrangement for them both."

"And what is it we're supposed to find here?"

"That," said Double Helix, drawing to a halt. Ahead of them was a large oval stadium; the curved walls made it look more like a discarded piece of giant fruit. "This particular city was once the secret lair of a wonderful villain who went by the name Dr Extar." He raised his eyebrows and shrugged. "It was the 1960s, and you could get away with calling yourself pretty much anything then, as long as it sounded sci-fi enough. The World Consortium murdered him, and this, his legacy, was crushed and hidden away from the world."

"No offence, but this place looks like a dump," said Kardach. "Why do you need it?"

Helix spun to face him. "What is the best way to control the world?"

"By force."

Helix gave a hollow laugh. "No. That is the quickest way to get spotted and defeated. The best and most efficient way is by stealth. Right now the World Consortium controls the world. All those other governments, they're just puppets who fall into line. And when they don't... Well, you see those countries on the news all the time. They are the ones always struggling; they always seem to be at war. There are more than enough criminal organizations that try to use brute force to get their way. And they *always* fail. They're idiots who never get the message. If you want to control the world, you don't tell *anybody* about it."

"But won't people notice if someone takes over the world?"

Double Helix replied with an enigmatic smile. "People believe whatever they want to believe."

With that, he continued walking towards the stadium.

DRONING ON

Avoiding the Shadow Helix guards in the freighter's long passageways looked to be a straightforward task. Dev had performed his usual trick on the security cameras mounted at every junction, and they guessed that there weren't enough crew to perform a thorough search.

The teens made their way down a few decks, Lot's stolen key card opening every locked passage door. Then they circled around and upwards, hoping they were doubling back on themselves. A few times Dev had stopped and shushed them as he heard the dull footfalls of search parties on the decks above or below them.

Eventually, Mason hauled a heavy steel bulkhead

door open and they felt a blast of fresh sea air. "I think we're back on the deck."

They sneaked out, crouching behind a pile of rope and metal cases lashed to the deck. Beyond they could see two guards at the gangplank.

"Piece of cake," chuckled Mason.

A mosquito-like whine caught Lot's attention, and she slowly turned around. Hovering behind them was a tiny drone, about the size of a thumb. The iris on the small camera spiralled open as it focused on them, and a tiny, pencil-thin cannon aimed at her.

Lot moved on instinct, thrusting the taser – which she had grimly wielded the moment they had gone on the run – at the drone. The electric charge exploded one of the four small turbine engines, and the drone slewed sideways as it fired its cute little cannon.

Lot had expected the tiny missile to have the savagery of a pea-shooter. Instead it exploded against the deck with enough power to blow up a car.

The deck shuddered, and the two guards drew their energy rifles, but they didn't move from their station.

Lot followed through with a high kick to the drone – which struck the bulkhead and pathetically snapped in half.

Dev was baffled as to why the guards didn't close in. He was answered a moment later by a loud buzz as a swarm of hundreds of tiny drones soared into view like an angry black cloud. It was no wonder Shadow Helix didn't bother to search the freighter. He had seen such swarm behaviour before in the Inventory and had even played with a group of microbots designed to mimic a swarm of ants in order to repair objects.

He hoped that, like most military applications, these drones had a built-in sense of self-protection. "Run!" he bellowed, leading a charge towards the two guards.

The guards opened fire. Their first volleys were warning shots, intended to fall wide, but instead they accidentally struck several drones, blasting them from the sky.

That's what Dev had been hoping for. He suddenly veered sideways, drawing Lot and Mason with him.

His timing was impeccable. Sensing a more immediate threat than the escaping prisoners, the drones turned their collective firepower on to the guards. Dozens of miniature high-powered missiles were launched at the confused guards.

The resulting explosion shook the freighter once again. Dev, Lot and Mason didn't dare turn around, dreading what they'd see. Instead, Dev directed them towards the nearest lifeboat. They tumbled inside.

Dev stretched out for the crane control, and his power leeched through the simple computer system, ordering it to drop the boat.

The brakes on the crane's cable immediately released, and the boat dropped down the side of the freighter. The movement was so sudden that his hand had been snatched away before he had time to instruct the crane to slow down to a stop before they reached the bottom. Dev braced himself for a violent splashdown.

It didn't come. He'd misjudged that too. This section of the freighter was docked against the city. Smoke streamed from the winch on the deck, the friction of which was the only thing slowing the lifeboat down as it slammed into the city's quay.

The impact caused the small boat to bounce and roll multiple times – its passengers clinging on to the seats for their lives – before the craft slid to a halt in a stream of sparks.

Dev's head was spinning as he sat up. His vision blurred, and his hand automatically went to his nose because he could smell the iron scent of blood. He was bleeding, and he guessed it wasn't from the impact.

How much time did Dev have left before his uncle's assassination worked? He didn't know; part of him no longer cared. He just wanted to prove his friends' innocence and stop Double Helix in his tracks. Beyond that, nothing else mattered.

Lot's voice cut through his thoughts. "They're still coming!"

Dev rubbed his eyes. His focus slowly came back, enough to see Lot and Mason standing at the prow of the stricken lifeboat, pointing to an ominous black cloud of killer drones that descended from the freighter.

A sense of panic seized Dev as he stumbled to his feet. "Run!"

He vaulted over the side of the boat, the others close behind him, and sprinted into the city streets. He had a vague notion of trying to lose the drones amongst the labyrinth of buildings, but he wasn't sure how.

He rounded a corner, then glanced behind as the swarm buzzed into view, rapidly catching up. Within moments they'd be within firing range, and Dev was out of options. Out in the open, in the middle of the street, they were sitting ducks.

"Do something!" yelled Lot with rising panic.

Dev stopped and threw the kitbag down in

frustration. "There's nothing but rubbish in here! I mean, we can throw a drink at them?"

Mason's face lit up. "Brilliant!" He rummaged through the bag. "Remember the soup!"

Lot shook her head, confused. "Mase, stop messing about! They're getting closer."

Mason pulled out the EverFrost flask, wound up his arm, then hurled it in a perfect rugby spin throw. The flask shot through the air straight and true.

"That's not going to do anything—" Dev began, expecting a couple of drones to be knocked from the sky, at best. Instead the swarm reacted by shooting the incoming projectile out of the way.

The tiny missile struck its target. The flask exploded in a blizzard of rapidly expanding frozen particles that froze in a huge cloud of fluffy ice – snagging the swarm in a frozen death grip.

Then the whole cloud came crashing down, crumpling apart like a snowball and crushing the drones with it.

Lot and Mason whooped loudly – jumping up and down, victorious. Mason pumped his fist in the air. "Yeah! Iced them!" he yelled.

Their moment of jubilation was punctured when Dev

was yet again overcome with dizziness and dropped to his hands and knees. Lot and Mason ran to his side.

"Mate! Talk to me."

Dev felt his chest constricting. His throat felt dry, and he struggled to find the words. "Mason . . . that was smart thinking."

Mason looked at Lot with concern. "I think we're losing him. He just complimented me."

Dev shoved Mason away and placed his palms on the floor, this time not for balance, but because he sensed something as he fell. He was vaguely aware that Lot was talking with concern, but he tuned her out as his synaesthesia reacted to the floor. It was the first time it had ever triggered with no conscious effort from himself. It was a different sensation than usual, and he wondered if this was a side effect from his impending doom.

He spread his fingers and closed his eyes. An aurora of power resonated not just through the floor, but the entire city. Every building and every surface was alive with pulses of energy.

"Dev?" said Lot. "Get up."

"You can't see it. . ." Dev finally managed. "But this . . . all of this. . . It's not a city." He stood up, regarding the buildings around them with fresh eyes.

"Looks like a city to me," said Mason doubtfully. "A really freaky one, but. . ."

"It's a machine. All of it. *One giant machine*." With the revelation came a knowledge rising from deep within his mind. But it wasn't his own memory — and he was starting to wonder just how many memories Professor Liu had implanted.

NEVERMIND

As they approached the stadium structure, the name of the building popped into Dev's memory.

"The *synchro-cogitron*," he said, with a hint of annoyance. Remembering the name was very different from knowing how it worked. "They called this place Project Nevermind..."

Suddenly, a loud crump echoed across the city, as if a giant switch had been thrown, and a slow whirling noise rose from the synchro-cogitron.

There were no doors or windows on the building, only a single tunnel entrance. "That looks like the only way in," said Lot, pointing to it.

"Looks like a trap to me," said Mason. "Tell me the old man had a plan for this that he zapped into your brain?"

Dev also hoped Professor Liu had a plan on how to stop Double Helix, but right now his memory wasn't sharing it. "I'm sure I'll remember things as things happen." It wasn't the assurance the others wanted, and he wasn't entirely sure he believed it either, but they had no choice but to move forward.

As they drew near, the air began to smell of electricity and sparks shot along the top of the stadium walls, each with the short snap of an embarrassed thunderclap.

"Look at that!" exclaimed Mason, his head cranked upwards.

A green aurora rose from the stadium, reaching for the clear sky. As it stretched higher, the colours began to change to purples and reds. The pulsing tone from within the synchro-cogitron increased, and so did the intensity of the lights.

Dev hurried them into the tunnel. He'd never been to a football ground before, but he'd seen footage on TV of the players emerging into a floodlit stadium.

It was very much like that, except the interior of this stadium didn't have a pitch. Instead, it had a central platform with five curving towers stretching upwards from it like a claw. It was from the "fingers" that the aurora energy was discharging.

Pipes and cables covered the floor like cooked spaghetti, connecting to a massive circular machine that ran around them, where Dev imagined the stadium seating should be. Unlike the simple linearity of the Large Hadron Collider, this machine had dozens of pipes, curled and twisted over one another in a complex knot.

The three figures on the platform didn't spot Dev, Lot and Mason, who hid behind a chunk of machinery. They risked poking their heads up for a better look as the entire structure around them began to vibrate.

Double Helix stood at the centre of the platform, a metal crown around his head. This wasn't one of gold and diamonds, but of rare elements and twisted engineering. As Dev watched, more memories flooded into his conscious.

"It's tapping into his thoughts... The synchro-cogitron amplifies them." He saw the look Lot was giving him. "Professor Liu helped make this..."

Mason was confused. "Wait, I thought he was one of the good guys, working for the Inventory? Wasn't this owned by Dr What's-his-face?"

"That doesn't matter," said Lot urgently. "We've got to stop . . . whatever it is he's doing."

"The synchro-cogitron implants thoughts." Dev's hand touched the TelePath in his pocket; it was the little brother of the monster in front of them. But the synchro-cogitron had a more nefarious purpose than simply allowing short-range telepathic communication. "It converts his thoughts into energy pulses that bounce off the ionosphere and seep into people's minds."

"So they think what he thinks?"

"Not quite. Imagine dispersing a single idea, such as 'obey me' – and people will just do it without question. Without knowing why."

"Conquering the world and still nobody will be any the wiser," said Lot.

"And nobody will even think of stopping him."

"So do you happen to remember where the off button is?"

Dev peeked again. The aurora intensity had dramatically increased. Above them, the kaleidoscope of energy was now spreading in every direction as it struck the ionosphere. On the platform, the Collector was intently watching dials and oscilloscopes on a control panel, while Kardach craned his neck upwards in awe.

New memories flooded into Dev's mind. "There is no way of powering it down. That's why this place was shrunk in the first place. We need that." He pointed at the Newton's Arrow strapped to Kardach's back.

Kardach knew the basics of the plan. He understood that a simple suggestive nudge could send people's lives in one direction, or even make them do things they never would. Like Christen Sandberg, they had to be weak-minded fools.

Then another thought nagged him: had Helix and the Collector used such technology on *him*?

Impossible. He cast that notion aside.

He thought he saw movement in the machinery at the edge of the platform. Staring at the bright aurora above had made his eyes water, so he wasn't sure whether it was just a trick of the eyes...

No – there it was again. The brats were surely out of action by now, back on the freighter. Could it be a crewman? They had been ordered to stay on the ship, and nobody would dare disobey an order from Double Helix ... would they?

Double Helix had his eyes tightly closed as the

synchro-cogitron sucked thoughts from his brain. From his expression, it was a painful process.

The Collector was staring intently at the controls, so Kardach didn't dare disturb him.

Curious, Kardach stepped off the platform. Yes, there was a crewman standing to attention in the shadows.

"What are you doing here?"

"I came to see if there was anything you needed, sir."

Kardach frowned, his suspicion rising. The crewman seemed uncertain. In fact, the closer he got, the more the man seemed to blur. Kardach rubbed his eyes; staring at the aurora had really affected his vision. When he looked up again, the image of the crewman fizzled, his features resolving into those of a young boy. . .

"Dammit!" said Mason, frantically tapping his BlurBadge as it struggled to function amid interference from the powerful machinery nearby.

Kardach tensed, poised to lunge for the boy — when he felt a terrible stabbing pain in his side. Lot had emerged from the shadows, discharging the taser in his rib cage. Kardach was unconscious before he struck the ground.

Dev slipped in behind Lot and stooped over Kardach, retrieving Newton's Arrow with a grunt.

"Try and Wi-Fi me now," Dev taunted under his breath, checking they hadn't been spotted as he placed the strap over his neck and took a moment to savour his success in retrieving it.

He connected to the weapon again, exploring its inner workings, coaxing the gadget to reveal its secrets. Unlike last time, he received more information – likely in combination with hidden memories that Professor Liu had planted. After all, the old man had designed the weapon. He of all people should know what it was capable of.

Dev activated Newton's Arrow. He felt the power tremble through the weapon as the gravitons spooled up in the repaired graviton pod, increasing the mass of the weapon. He turned the gun towards the platform and considered yelling some sort of warning, so they would know all too well who would defeat them, but the devil on his shoulder told him, *why bother?* All the pain, heartache and his rapidly approaching death were all due to the two figures standing before him. He didn't owe them anything.

He pulled the trigger.

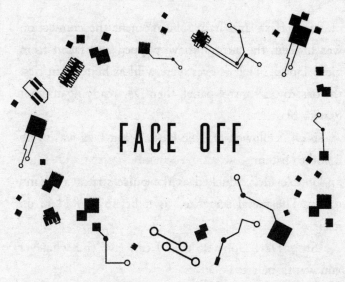

FACE OFF

The recoil in the rifle was more than Dev had anticipated. The gravity stream shot out at an angle, striking the control desk. The Collector back-pedalled as the entire control panel began to fold into itself. As nothing else around it was shrinking, the controls tore themselves away from the surrounding platform in a shower of sparks – followed by a huge explosion that tunnelled down into the platform. One of the five extended metal fingers was engulfed in flame and came crashing down, close to Double Helix.

Double Helix screamed in pain, yanking the crown off. Where it had rested on his head was now a band of burnt flesh and hair. The moment the connection was broken, the aurora above popped and faded from view. Double Helix's eyes were wild as he took in first the destroyed control panel, then Dev readying another gravity blast.

"NO!" bellowed Double Helix – but Dev was in no mood to listen.

Double Helix ducked as the pulse struck a second tower. The metal screeched as it began to fold in on itself.

"Stop, Dev! Don't do this. I can give you whatever you want," he cried.

"I know you can," called out Dev, straining under the rifle's weight, "because one of the things I want is you out of my life!"

Dev increased the charge on the Arrow. He knew what he had to do next; Professor Liu had planted it in his mind already.

Double Helix's voice rose with an edge of hysteria. "I can stop the Dissolution Protocol, Dev. I can help you to live!"

"Impossible." His uncle had created the system; it was a one-way process. That's what he had been told. But he had been lied to before. "You told me that."

"Your uncle created it . . . but I know how. And I can reverse it."

Dev's finger hesitated over the trigger. The chance for life. . . How could he refuse such an offer? He glanced around and saw Lot and Mason watching him carefully. Then he noticed that the Collector had vanished, *like a coward*.

Double Helix raised his hands in surrender. "I told you, never believe your eyes, Dev." Double Helix took a step forward, but stopped when Dev raised the weapon menacingly. "When people look at me they only see what they want to see."

Double Helix looked at Mason, who was standing back, a few metres beyond Dev. "What colour is my hair?"

"Black," replied Mason, slightly puzzled.

Dev threw a look at Mason, but didn't divert his aim on Double Helix. "Are you colour-blind or something? He's blond!"

"No, he's bald," Lot chimed in.

The three of them exchanged confused looks, then turned their attention to Double Helix once again.

Helix pointed to Mason. "A BlurBadge. Very good. There are better methods of changing your appearance." He held up his wrist, which had a thin bracelet hanging around it. "A Janus bracelet. Named after a Roman god. Very useful. Think of it as a cloaking shield, like the one on your aircraft. It makes you appear however it is you want others to see you, however they interpret the message. In my case, it's anonymity. Only one other person knows my true appearance."

"And I bet you killed them?"

"No." Helix moved his other hand slowly and deliberately. He tapped on the wristband, and lights flickered over its narrow surface as it deactivated.

Dev lowered the gun in surprise. The man standing before him was—

"Charles Parker?" Mason exclaimed in shock.

One moment Helix had looked like a normal, nondescript man, then he suddenly looked like Charles. There was no transition, no morphing of features, just a sharp switch.

"It's a trick," said Lot. "He's stalling for time."

"It's not a trick. Double Helix ... you never questioned the name?"

Dev shook his head in response.

"Charles and I were twins. Conjoined twins, to be precise. When we were born, Charles was the more fully formed. I was fused to his back like a parasite."

Double Helix bent his knee and rolled up his trouser leg, revealing the skin beneath. "I was surgically removed. Your uncle kept the important things, like his own limbs. I had only one arm and a single leg."

He tore the skin from his shin away. It was nothing more than silicone. Beneath it was a cybernetic limb crafted from sleek, polished metal.

"I was discarded in the trash. I would have been incinerated, but I refused to die. While your uncle went on to have an illustrious career, I was cast to the shadows." He gestured to the synchro-cogitron around him. "This was my revenge on the world. With the technology I stole from under my brother's nose, I would be able to run the world. Why enslave people when they could still go about their mundane lives – making money and paying their taxes, all of which eventually goes to the rich businessmen who pull the population's strings. Whereas I pull the strings of the elite."

"All that to prove you're just as worthy as my uncle?"

Double Helix laughed. "No. All of that just for *fun*. Watching Charles's life collapse as I take everything from him – that's my revenge." He extended his hand in a friendly gesture. "You hate him as much as I. He passed a death sentence on you. Did I do such a thing?

No. Did I harm your friends? No. Think, Dev, who is your real enemy in all of this?"

Dev looked at Lot and Mason – then tossed Newton's Arrow to the floor.

Lot was horrified. "Dev! No! What are you doing?"

Dev's smile was so ruthless and calculating that he noticed Lot take a step backwards in fear.

"What am I doing? I'm taking a leaf out of his book." He pointed to Double Helix. The villain smiled and lowered his hands.

"I knew you would see sense, Devon."

Devon continued talking to Lot. "And in Double Helix's book there is one major rule – always plan a step ahead." He turned to Double Helix. "And don't ever call me *Devon*."

Double Helix's gaze fell to Dev's *other* hand. He was holding the graviton pod, ejected the same moment he had cast aside the gun. And if there was one memory Dev had inherited, it was *never to eject a graviton pod when it was at full charge*.

With all his strength, he hurled the pod at one of the three remaining towers.

"RUN!" he ordered, stooping only to retrieve Newton's Arrow from the floor.

Mason and Lot were already ahead of him. The pod shattered, unleashing a swirling mass of gravitons that formed a miniature black hole, suspended in space.

By the time they reached the tunnel, the towers were all bent towards the black hole – stretching into fine tendrils as they were sucked into the gravity vortex, one atom at a time. It was a chain reaction: as it swallowed the synchro-cogitron, the black hole grew bigger, gobbling up even more.

As Dev, Lot and Mason charged from the tunnel, the stadium was twisting like melted toffee as the black hole consumed it.

"Run for the ship!" shouted Dev as the wind began to whip up around them in a gale. The swelling black hole inhaled the very air around them. With every three steps they took, the wind seemed to push them back one.

"This is hopeless!" Lot wailed.

The ground began to shake violently. The trio stopped in their tracks, clinging on to the side of a building for support. Above them, the tops of the skyscrapers bent like trees in a hurricane – the gravity force seemed to be stronger up there. The sound of wrenching metal came from ahead. Something was rapidly heading their way.

"I've got a bad feeling about—" Mason started to say before he was cut off. The Shadow Helix freighter crashed through the base of the tower in front of them. Debris didn't have time to fall back to earth before they spiralled past the teens into the vortex behind them.

The freighter's hull scraped along the street in a massive shower of sparks, and the entire ship listed at a forty-degree angle as it was dragged inexorably towards the black hole.

Dev pointed to the angled deck. "There's our only chance!"

The Avro was still locked in place by the giant claw mechanism. As the freighter rumbled past them, they saw that the mangled gangplank was still attached. The tongue of metal was crushed and bent, as the weight of the ship had fallen on it, but it offered a route to scramble on to the deck.

They ran almost doubled over to minimize the effects of the wind rushing towards the void. Lot was the first to reach the gangplank, scrambling on-board on all fours. Dev followed, pausing to help pull Mason up as the fragile gangplank buckled under his weight.

The smooth, steep deck was difficult to climb. Dev was thankful it wasn't wet; he doubted they could have made it otherwise. They reached the helipad, the underpinning support gantry providing ideal handholds for them to clamber up towards the Avro's ramp.

The trembling motion of the freighter suddenly changed as the prow drew closer to the yawning black hole, which now looked like a buzz-saw blade as it lazily spun a debris field that increased in size as it chewed the island up. As gravity acted upon the freighter, the prow began to stretch in countless strands towards the void.

Lot reached the Avro's ramp, and Dev felt a thrill of hope. They were going to make it. The thrill rapidly changed to wooziness, and he felt another trickle of blood from his nose.

Mason's voice sounded distant. "Deeeevvv!!"

Dev felt his fingers weaken, and the steel girder he was clinging to slipped from his grasp. Then he was falling. He slammed into the inclined deck and shot head first back the way they'd come. Straight off the edge of the deck—

A sharp pain on his shoulder snapped him out of his malaise. The strap from Newton's Arrow had snagged on a twisted part of the gunwale that had been blown away by the security drone. Dev was suspended over the drop, his legs cycling uselessly. He tried to pull himself up, but his arms trembled and he had no strength left.

A third of the freighter had gone already, and the superstructure now looked like a snarl of flailing squid tentacles as it was pulled inside the black hole. Dev saw Lot on the Avro's ramp, Mason clinging to the helipad just beneath her. He knew for certain he didn't have the strength to reach them.

"Go!" he bellowed, shooing them with his arm.

Lot and Mason exchanged words, but Dev couldn't hear them. His head felt like cotton wool, and he struggled to stay awake. It was a race between death by black hole or by his uncle's self-destruct protocol. *It could well be a draw*, Dev thought bleakly.

When he looked up again, he saw that the disc was powering up, and straining against the clamps that held it in place. Good for Lot, Dev thought; at least she'd be able to take Mason to safety. Dev allowed himself to hang limply from the strap; there was no use fighting whatever fate had in store for him.

The Avro pushed against the metal claws that held it in place. Dev could see the metal clamps shudder – but still they held.

"Go on, Lot!" he yelled, but knew she couldn't hear him.

Again the Avro pushed against its restraints, but went nowhere and settled back on the pad. Dev didn't believe for a moment that Lot would give up.

And he was right.

The Avro rose once more, but this time it began to spin, rapidly building speed until — like a buzz-saw blade — it struck the clamps. Sparks flew as the metal claws were torn in half, and with it sections of the aircraft's hull. But it didn't matter — Dev cheered as the Avro shot free.

But instead of flying to safety, the Avro arced overhead and banked low next to the freighter. Then a yell of thrilled terror drew Dev's attention back to the deck. Mason hadn't boarded the aircraft after all. He slid down the incline — straight for Dev. And he wasn't going to stop.

Mason cannonballed into Dev so hard that the metal holding Dev in place snapped, and they both fell. . .

But not far. They landed on the top of the Avro, which Lot was skilfully piloting metres off the ground — a task made all the harder by the thick, black smoke issuing from the fresh gouge in the fuselage and being sucked past the viewport by the black hole.

Mason threw one arm around Dev to secure his

friend, the other gripping the sunken rungs of the access ladder running across the hull.

"We don't leave a man behind!" laughed Mason as the Avro pulled into a sharp climb. Dev glanced behind as they accelerated away. He watched as the remains of the freighter were swallowed up seconds later.

The black hole was gaining critical mass now, exactly as his implanted memories predicted it would. In seconds the rest of the city folded into the throat of the gravity monster. Then the black hole twisted shape as it began to consume itself.

With an unspectacular *POP!* the black hole folded in on itself and crunched into nothingness . . . leaving only a silent ocean behind.

The Avro quivered as more smoke spewed from the gouge and they rapidly lost altitude. Mason and Dev could only hold on tight as Lot landed on the water, skipping four times, like a stone, before slowing to a drifting stop, bobbing atop of the ocean surface.

An access hatch opened, and Lot scrambled through. "We've lost all power." She kneeled next to Dev. "How're you feeling?"

Dev didn't answer. The aircraft's soft, rocking motion on the waves was lulling him into darkness. . .

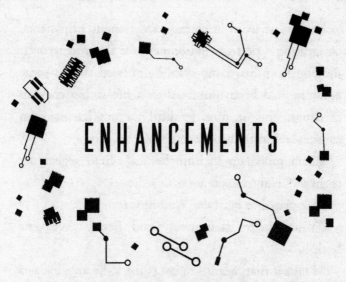

ENHANCEMENTS

The light hurt Dev's eyes as he opened them. He'd heard tales of people surviving near-death experiences and seeing bright lights at the end of a tunnel, but he very much doubted any afterlife would look like the clinically white walls of the Inventory medical bay.

He sat up – and banged his head on a Perspex canopy, which almost knocked him back unconscious.

"Easy," came Eema's voice.

The canopy opened with a hiss, allowing Dev to slowly sit upright, dangling his legs off the side of the pod he had been lying in. He knew about the BioPods, although he'd never been in one. They were supposed to be the last word in curing exceptionally ill patients, by creating a perfect environment for them to recover. Judging from his damp skin, he guessed that at some point he had been immersed in a life-saving cocktail of drugs, and he was thankful for not having been conscious during that process.

Eema rolled up to him, her holo-head registering concern. "How do you feel?"

"Surprised to be alive." And he was.

"You're better than new," said Eema. "Welcome back."

"I take it that means I'm not going to be arrested as a traitor, then?"

Charles Parker entered the room and stood next to Eema, his arms folded. "Not at all, Dev. You did what you were asked. We have Newton's Arrow back, and it's safely stored in the Red Zone."

Dev couldn't help but notice his uncle's first words were all business; he hadn't even acknowledged Dev's condition.

"So you won't be activating my self-destruct again?" From his uncle's expression, it was clear Charles was unsure just how much Dev knew. "Oh, I had a long talk with your evil twin." Dev took some satisfaction at the panicked look that crossed his uncle's face. "He had a lot to say. Speaking of which, where are Lot and Mason?"

Charles could hardly find his voice to speak. "They're waiting for you," he finally said.

Dev jumped off the bed, only then realizing he was wearing a hospital gown. His dirty clothes lay on a chair in the corner. He looked his uncle straight in the eye. "So why didn't your precious Dissolution Protocol kill me after all?"

"It seems when you used synaesthesia on an active particle accelerator, it changed something inside of you."

Dev knew his uncle was holding something back, but he didn't have the energy for an argument. He was just happy to be alive. "Did you find any signs of Double Helix? Kardach? The Collector?"

"Sergeant Wade arrived moments after you blacked out. Luckily, they had seen the smoke from the Avro. She conducted a thorough search of the area afterwards, but found nothing. However, Consortium satellites detected a strong energy signal from the area moments before the vortex collapsed on itself."

"Meaning they could have got away?"

Charles shrugged. "We may not understand the energy signature of these kinds of phenomena as well as we think. On the other hand, we know parasites are very hard to kill." Then he placed his hand on Dev's shoulder. It was an awkward gesture. "Devon, I am so pleased you're back. We shouldn't have jumped to conclusions about you."

"No, you shouldn't have." Dev slipped his uncle's hand off his shoulder and began to dress in his own clothes. He had been surprised by his uncle's gesture; but rather than make him happy, it angered him.

Too little too late, he thought.

In the canteen, Dev was crushed by Lot and Mason in a tight hug. They were delighted to see him up. Mason joked that he'd been jealous that Dev missed several more days' worth of school than they had, but assured him not much had changed there.

Even more unexpected was the round of applause from dozens of Inventory technicians, led by Sergeant Wade.

"You should have seen the naval fleet Sarge led to find us," said Mason excitedly as they detailed the story of Wade picking them up from the ocean.

Wade congratulated them all on an amazing job — not only in retrieving the artefact, but also bringing

Shadow Helix down. It was a phenomenal achievement. Dev wondered just how much Wade knew about Uncle Parker and Double Helix's connection, as nothing about it was said. Lot and Mason must have been thinking the same thing, but they too kept that nugget of information quiet.

"The only downside so far is the incident in Hong Kong," said Wade. "The city is a mess. Gravity decided to revert to normal twenty-six hours ago, and everything came crashing down. Luckily the authorities had evacuated everybody. But here's the thing: a lot of people there have already forgotten what happened."

Dev thought about that. "Well, Hong Kong wasn't *that* far from where Double Helix activated Project Nevermind. He was always talking about conquest by stealth, so he wouldn't have wanted people knowing about all that tech. Could he have implanted the thought for them to forget what had happened?"

"It seems that the aurora had time to travel that far, so I suppose that could make sense. The rest of the world is still talking about aliens, but we have set a good disinformation campaign in motion, blaming it on natural events. People will soon forget. They always do. My concern is what other message Double Helix was trying to get out to the world."

So their catch-up continued, with Wade almost casually dropping in the news that Professor Liu had passed away in Hong Kong's aftermath. Dev felt incredibly saddened by the news, although he wasn't too sure if that was more an effect of sharing the old man's memories. He wondered whether the professor had planted more things in Dev's subconscious than he was aware of.

He touched the TelePath in his pocket. It had survived the madness in the city, and he had no intention of declaring it to his uncle. It wasn't the Inventory's gadget, it was his very own. His first. And he intended to use it.

The conversation changed to the improved security measures in the Inventory, now that they had the first Red Zone artefact back. On a holo-screen, Wade showed them the complex's layout, and she highlighted the various improvements, but Dev wasn't really listening. He was searching the map, wondering where Charles had triggered the Dissolution Protocol. He had surfed the Inventory's computers for long enough to know that it wasn't part of the main system. Did that mean there was a secret place he didn't know about?

There was nothing there.

Storage closets, air-conditioning vents and toilets were all marked up, but the chamber that had almost led to his death wasn't there.

He examined the curving corridors, and the various colour-coordinated warehouses nested into one another, but the map revealed nothing. Then the Collector's words came back, uttered in Tartarus Prison.

The Black Zone. . . But there was no black zone. Had he made it up, just to sow confusion?

Then Dev saw it. A simple optical illusion, like when an image of two faces suddenly becomes a vase. You can see the faces or the vase – but not both, and he had been looking at the map in just one way. The map with huge concentric black spaces between the corridors, an area that took up almost a third of the Inventory's space.

A zone within a zone.

Dev felt the familiar sensation of curiosity bubbling inside of him. It seemed that the Inventory had many more secrets left to tell. . .

Andy Briggs is a screenwriter,
graphic novelist, author
and conservationist.

Follow him online:

andybriggs.co.uk
@abriggswriter